PRAISE FOR ETGAR KERET

"I read [*The Nimrod Flipout*] in bed beside my boyfriend who was reading a much less interesting book and I kept shouting 'Wow' and 'No way' and 'Oh my god' and my boyfriend would say, 'What? what?' and I'd shake my head and say, 'You wouldn't get it. You just have to read it.' After I finished the book I immediately became more deadpan, more ridiculous and more in touch with my own mortality. My boyfriend was impressed with the new me and I told him, 'It's that book, *The Nimrod Flipout*—it's opened up a whole new world for me.' Now he's reading it, just so we can stay on the same plane of reality together."

—Miranda July, *Salon*

"Etgar Keret's short stories are fierce, funny, full of energy and insight, and at the same time often deep, tragic, and very moving."

—Amos Oz, author of *A Tale of Love and Darkness*

"Keret is a cynic who can't manage to shake off his hopefulness— the most reliable kind of narrator there is . . . To call Keret apolitical would be to miss a seminal moment in the history of Jewish literature. Indeed, it would be like pigeonholing Isaac Bashevis Singer—at whose knee Keret seems to have learned the art of magic realism, only to use it with more discipline than his master."

—Alana Newhouse, *The Washington Post Book World*

"If there were a fiction genre combining wit, wild imagination, penetrating insights, fantasy (sexual and otherwise) and the paranormal, Keret would dominate it like Stephen King dominates horror . . . Keret's a strange genius."

—Kevin Walker, *The Tampa Tribune*

ETGAR KERET

THE GIRL ON THE FRIDGE

Born in Tel Aviv in 1967, Etgar Keret is the author of five best-selling collections. In America his stories have been featured on *This American Life* and *Selected Shorts*. As screenwriter-directors, he and his wife, Shira Geffen, shared the Caméra d'Or for best debut feature (*Jellyfish*) at the 2007 Cannes Film Festival.

THE GIRL ON THE FRIDGE

THE GIRL ON THE FRIDGE

ETGAR KERET

Translated from the Hebrew by
Miriam Shlesinger and Sondra Silverston

FARRAR, STRAUS AND GIROUX · NEW YORK

FARRAR, STRAUS AND GIROUX
18 West 18th Street, New York 10011

Some of these translations previously appeared, in slightly
different form, in *Bomb*, *LA Weekly*, *The Paris Review*, *Tin House*, and
Words Without Borders.

Library of Congress Cataloging-in-Publication Data
Keret, Etgar, 1967–
    The girl on the fridge / Etgar Keret ; translated by Miriam
Shlesinger [and] Sondra Silverston. — 1st American ed.
        p.   cm.
      ISBN-13: 978-0-374-53105-8 (pbk. : alk. paper)
      ISBN-10: 0-374-53105-6 (pbk. : alk. paper)
    1. Keret, Etgar, 1967– —Translations into English.   I. Shlesinger,
Miriam, 1947–   II. Silverston, Sondra.   III. Title.

    PJ5054.K375G5713   2008
    892.4'36—dc22

                                                    2007047876

Designed by Gretchen Achilles

www.fsgbooks.com

1   3   5   7   9   10   8   6   4   2

CONTENTS

CONTENTS   vii

THE GIRL ON
THE FRIDGE

ASTHMA ATTACK

When you have an asthma attack, you can't breathe. When you can't breathe, you can hardly talk. To make a sentence all you get is the air in your lungs. Which isn't much. Three to six words, if that. You learn the value of words. You rummage through the jumble in your head. Choose the crucial ones—those cost you too. Let healthy people toss out whatever comes to mind, the way you throw out the garbage. When an asthmatic says "I love you," and when an asthmatic says "I love you madly," there's a difference. The difference of a word. A word's a lot. It could be *stop*, or *inhaler*. It could even be *ambulance*.

CRAZY GLUE

She said, "Don't touch it," and I asked, "What is it?"

"It's glue," she said. "Special glue. Superglue."

And I asked: "What did you buy that for?"

"Because I need it," she said. "I've got lots of things to glue together."

"There's nothing that needs gluing together," I snapped. "I can't understand why you buy all this crap."

"The same reason I married you," she shot back, "to kill time."

I didn't feel like getting into a fight, so I kept quiet, and so did she. "Is it any good, this glue?" I asked. She showed me the picture on the box, with this guy hanging upside down from the ceiling after someone had smeared some glue on the soles of his shoes.

"No glue can make a person stick like that," I said. "They took the picture upside down. He's standing on the floor. They just stuck a light fixture in the floor to make it look like a ceiling. You can tell right away by the way the window looks. They put the clasp on the blinds backwards. Take a look." I pointed at the window in the picture. She didn't look. "It's eight already," I said, "I've got to run." I picked up my briefcase and kissed her on the cheek. "I'll be back late. I'm—"

"I know," she snapped. "You're swamped."

I called Mindy from the office. "I can't make it today," I said. "I've got to be home early."

"How come? Is anything the matter?"

"No. I mean, yeah. I think she suspects something." There was a long silence. I could hear Mindy breathing on the other end.

"I don't see why you stay with her," she whispered in the end. "The two of you never do anything. You don't even bother fighting anymore. I can't figure out why you go on like this. I just don't get what's holding you together. I don't get it," she said again. "I simply don't get it . . ." and she started crying.

"Don't cry, Mindy," I told her. "Listen," I lied. "Somebody just came in. I've got to go. I'll come over tomorrow, promise. We'll talk then."

I got home early. I called out hello when I walked in the door, but there was no reply. I went from room to room. She wasn't in any of them. On the kitchen table I found the tube of glue, completely empty. I tried to pull one of the chairs out, to sit down. It didn't budge. I tried again. Stuck. She'd glued it to the floor. The fridge wouldn't open. She'd glued it shut. I couldn't see why she'd pull a stunt like this. She'd always seemed reasonably sane. This just wasn't like her. I went into the living room to get the phone. I thought she might have gone to her mother's. I couldn't lift the receiver. She'd glued that down too. Furious, I kicked at the telephone table and almost broke my toe. The table didn't budge.

That's when I heard her laughing. It was coming from up above me. I looked, and there she was, hanging upside down, her bare feet clinging to the high living room ceiling. I looked at her, stunned. "What the fuck. Have you lost your mind?" She didn't answer, just smiled. Her smile seemed so natural, the way she was hanging, as if just her lips were subject to gravity. "Don't worry," I said. "I'll get you down," and I pulled some books off the shelf. I stacked up a few volumes of the encyclopedia and got on top of the pile. "This may hurt a little," I said, trying to keep my balance. She went on smiling. I pulled as hard as I could, but nothing happened. Carefully, I climbed down. "Don't worry," I said. "I'll go to the neighbors to phone for help."

"Fine," she said and laughed. "I'm not going anywhere." By then I was laughing too. She was so pretty, and so incongruous, hanging upside down from the ceiling that way. With her long hair dangling downward, and her breasts molded like two perfect teardrops under her white T-shirt. So pretty. I climbed back up onto the pile of books and kissed her. I felt her tongue on mine. The books slipped out from under my feet as I hung there in midair, not touching a thing, dangling from just her lips.

LOQUAT

G o on, Henri, go talk to them. You're a *gendarme*, they'll listen to you."

I put down my empty coffee cup and moved my feet around under the table, trying to find my slippers. "How many times do I have to explain it to you, Grandma? I'm not a *gend*— a policeman. I'm a soldier, a *soldat*. I don't have anything to do with them, so why should they listen to what I have to say?"

"Because you're tall as a building and you wear a *gendarme*'s uniform—"

"*Soldat*, Grandma."

"So you're a *soldat*, what's the difference? You go to them with your *pistolet* and tell them that if they climb our loquat tree one more time, you'll throw them in the *calabouse* and shoot them, or something, just so they stop coming into our yard . . ."

Grandma's faded eyes were moist now, and bloodshot. She really hated those kids. The old lady wasn't all there, but out of respect I said okay. That evening, I heard them in the tree. I put on a pair of shorts and a sleeveless undershirt and told Grandma I was going out to talk to them.

"No," she said, blocking my way to the door, holding my ironed dress uniform. "You're not going out to them like that. Put on your uniform."

"Leave it alone, Grandma," I said, trying to get past her. She leaned against the door stubbornly, handing me my uniform.

"Your uniform," she said firmly.

I walked down the front steps, with her hopping down behind me. I felt mortified dressed up like a model soldier. She even made me wear the unit insignia. "Henri, you forgot this," she whispered in her raspy voice and held out the Uzi, loaded and cocked. If my commander had seen me then with my weapon in my hand, I'd have gotten two weeks inside.

I snatched the gun out of her hand, took out the magazine, and gently uncocked it. A bullet fell out of the muzzle onto the grass. "Why'd you bring me the gun, are you crazy? They're only kids."

I gave her the gun, but she slapped it right back into my hand. "That's not kids, that's animals," she said resolutely.

"Okay, Grandma, I'll take the rifle." I gave in with a hopeless sigh and kissed her cheek. "Now go inside."

"Oh, *mon petit gendarme*," Grandma said, clapping her hands happily. Filled with satisfaction at her small victory, she skipped up the steps.

"*Soldat*," I cried after her. "For fuck's sake, I'm not a fucking policeman." And I walked down the rest of the steps.

The kids in the loquat tree kept on making noise and breaking branches. I was planning to take off my shirt, wrap the rifle in it, and hide it in a bush so I'd look more or less normal when I went over to them, but the sight of Grandma's face peering out from behind a curtain stopped me. I walked over to a kid who was climbing the tree, grabbed him by the shirt, and pushed him onto the ground. *"Yallah,"* I yelled, "everyone out of the tree. This is private property."

There was a second of silence, then an answer came from one of the high branches. "Oh, I'm so scared. A soldier. You want to kill us, Mr. Soldier?" A rotten loquat hit me in the head.

The kid I'd pushed onto the ground got up and looked at me with contempt. "Paper pusher," he said. "My brother's in a combat patrol unit, working his ass off, and you're not ashamed to walk around with the insignia of that unit of pussies from Tel Aviv?" He brought up a gob of phlegm and spat on my shirt. I whacked him on the head hard enough to knock him down.

How the hell did the little schmuck know about insignias?

"Did you see that son of a bitch hit Meron?" someone yelled up in the tree.

"Hey, homo, what are you doing walking around in uniform on a Friday night?" another one shouted. "Can't you afford Levi's?"

"If he's so hot for the army, let's give him an intifada so he doesn't get bored," the first one shouted, and the one in the tree started throwing loquats. I tried to climb up to him, but it was next to impossible, what with the rifle and all.

Suddenly, a brick landed on my shoulder, and it turned out that there was another kid in the bushes. "PLO," he yelled and gave me the finger. Those kids were really fucked up. Before I could chase him, the kid who'd spat on me got up, his whole face covered with mud, kicked me in the balls, and started to run away. I saw red and caught up with him in about three steps. I pulled him by the shirt from behind and he fell. I started to beat on him. The one who threw the brick jumped onto my back, and two others came down from the tree to help him. They stuck to me like leeches. One of them bit me on the neck. I tried to shake them off and we all fell in the mud. I was punching them left and right. But those midget bastards had balls. They wouldn't give up no matter how much I hit them. I was holding one with each hand and was choking the third one with my legs when suddenly that Meron, who seemed to be their leader, smashed me in the head with a rock. The world spun, and I felt blood dripping onto my forehead. I heard a round of gunfire and noticed that I hadn't had the rifle for a while. It must have fallen when we were rolling around in the mud.

"Leave my grandson alone, *sales bêtes*." I heard my grandmother's voice. "Or else I'll finish you all off like carp in the bathtub."

I didn't know if it was real or I was dreaming. "Watch out, the old lady's crazy." I heard Meron's voice and felt all the hands letting go of me.

"And now get out of here, *tout de suite*," I heard my grandmother order them and then the sound of feet sloshing through mud.

"Look at how they dirtied your *gendarme* clothes," she said, and I could feel her hand on my shoulder. "And they split your head open," she continued her lament. "Never mind, I'll bandage you up and wash the clothes so they look like new. And God, he'll take care of those little devils. Come home, Henri, it's getting cold." I stood up, and the world kept spinning and spinning.

"Tell me, Grandma," I asked, "where'd you learn to load a gun and shoot like that?"

"From a Jacques Norris movie. It was on TV, before that cable bastard turned off the movies," she recalled angrily, "and ran away with my money. Tomorrow you'll wear your *gendarme* uniform and go pay him a visit too."

"Grandma!" I blurted out furiously, my forehead burning like hell.

"Sorry, Henri. *Soldat*," Grandma apologized and skipped up the steps.

HAT TRICK

At the end of the show, I pull a rabbit out of the hat. I always save it for last, because kids love animals. At least, when I was a kid I loved animals. That way the show ends on a high note, at the point when I pass the rabbit around so the kids can pet it and feed it. That's how it used to be. It's harder with kids nowadays. They don't get as excited, but still, I leave the rabbit for the end. It's the trick I love best. Or rather, it used to be. I'd keep my eyes fixed on the audience as my hand reached into the hat, groping deep inside it till it felt Kazam's ears.

And then "A-la-Kazeem—a-la-Kazam!" and out it comes. It never fails to surprise them. And not only them, me, too. Every time my hand touches those funny ears inside the hat I feel like a magician. And even though I know how it's done, the hollow space in the table and all that, it still seems like actual magic.

That Saturday afternoon in the suburbs I left the hat trick to the end, the way I always do. The kids at that birthday party were incredibly blasé. Some had their backs to me, watching a

Schwarzenegger movie on cable. The birthday boy wasn't even in the room, he was playing with his new video game. My audience had dwindled to a total of about four kids. It was especially hot that day. I was sweating like crazy under my magician's suit. All I wanted was to get through it and go home. I skipped over three rope tricks and went straight to the hat. My hand disappeared deep inside it, and my eyes sank into the eyes of a chubby girl with glasses. The soft touch of Kazam's ears took me by surprise the way it always does. "A-la-Kazeem—a-la-Kazam!" One more minute in the father's den and I was out of there, with a three-hundred-shekel check in my pocket. I pulled Kazam by the ears, and something about him felt a little strange, lighter. My hand swung up in the air, my eyes still fixed on the audience. And then—suddenly there was something wet on my wrist and the chubby girl started to scream. In my right hand I was holding Kazam's head, with his long ears and wide-open rabbit eyes. Just the head, no body. The head, and lots and lots of blood. The chubby girl kept screaming. The kids sitting with their backs to me turned away from the TV and started to clap. The birthday kid with the new video game came in from the other room and, when he saw the severed head, gave a loud whistle through his fingers. I could feel my lunch rising to my throat. I threw up into my magician's hat, and the vomit disappeared. The kids were ecstatic.

That night, I didn't sleep a wink. I kept checking my gear. I had no explanation at all for what had happened. Couldn't find the rest of Kazam either. In the morning, I went to the magicians' shop. They were baffled too. I bought a rabbit. The guy tried to sell me a turtle. "Rabbits are played," he told me. "Nowadays it's all about the turtles. Tell them it's a ninja, they'll freak."

I bought a rabbit anyway. I named it Kazam too. By the time I got home, there were five messages on my machine. All job offers. All from kids who'd witnessed the performance. One kid actually stipulated that I leave the severed head behind just like I'd done at the party. It was only then that I realized I hadn't taken Kazam's head with me.

My next gig was on Wednesday. A ten-year-old in Savyon Heights was having a birthday. I was stressed out all through the show. I couldn't get in the zone. I fucked up the Queen of Hearts trick. All I could think about was the hat. Finally it was time: "A-la-Kazeem—a-la-Kazam!" The penetrating look at the audience, the hand into the hat. I couldn't find the ears, but the body was the right weight. Smooth, but the right weight. And then the screaming again. Screaming, but also applause. It wasn't a rabbit I was holding, it was a dead baby.

I can't do that trick anymore. I used to love it, but just thinking about it now makes my hands shake. I keep imagining what terrible things I might wind up pulling out of there, the things waiting inside. Last night I dreamed I put my hand into the hat and it was caught in some creature's jaws. It baffles me how blithe I used to be about sticking my hand into that dark place. How blithe I was about shutting my eyes and sleeping.

I've stopped performing altogether, but I don't really care. I've stopped earning a living, but that's fine too. Sometimes I still put on the suit when I'm at home, for kicks, or I check the secret space in the table under the hat. That's about it. Apart from that, I pretty much stay away from magic tricks, I pretty much don't do anything. I just lie awake and think about the rabbit's head and the dead baby. Like they're clues to a riddle. It's as if someone was trying to tell me this is no time to be a rabbit, or a baby. Or a magician.

AN EXCLUSIVE

I was knocking down a wall.

All women reporters are whores and I was knocking down a wall. It was already something like four months since she'd left. At first, I thought all that manual labor would calm me down, but meanwhile it only upset me more. The wall I was knocking down had stood between the living room and the bedroom. So the balcony was always behind me. But I remembered. You don't have to see to remember. I remembered how we used to sit there at night.

"Look," she'd said, "a falling star. We have to make a wish. Come on," she'd said, kissing me on the neck, "wish for something."

"Okay, okay," I said, "I'm wishing."

"What did you wish?" she asked and tightened her arms around me. "Won't you tell me? Come on, tell me."

"That it'll always be like this, like it is now." I stroked her hair. "A breeze. The two of us together on the balcony."

"No," she said, pushing me away, "that's not a good wish. Wish for something else, something just for you."

"Okay, fine," I said with a laugh, "don't rush me. An FZR 1000. I wish for a Yamaha FZR 1000."

"A motorcycle?" She looked at me, shocked. "You get a wish and you ask for a motorcycle?"

"Yes," I said. "What did you wish for?"

"I'm not telling," she said, hiding her face in my sweater. "If you tell, it never comes true."

But if you don't tell, maybe it does. Two months later, she moved to Tel Aviv to work on one of the big dailies, nothing like the local rag in Hadera. She didn't say a word, one day she just disappeared. Her parents wouldn't give me her address. They said she didn't want to talk to me. "Why not?" I asked her father. "Did I hurt her feelings? Did I do something to her?"

"I don't know," he said, shrugging. "That's what she told me to say."

"Tell me, Mr. Brosh," I said, getting angry, "you think it's normal that your daughter and I have been going out together for two years, and all of a sudden, just like that, for no reason, she doesn't want to talk to me? You don't think I deserve an explanation?"

"That's not fair, Eli," her father said, leaning on the door handle. The whole conversation was taking place at the door to their apartment. "It really isn't fair," he said, running his hand over his bald head. "I'm not the one who left you, you know. I never did anything bad to you, right? I don't deserve for you to be taking that tone." He was right. That's all there was to it. I said I was sorry and left. Suddenly, he looked so forlorn. From then on, I tried to get to her through the paper. But they wouldn't give me her home number, and she was never at the office. So I left a message, I left a thousand messages, but she didn't call. A few months later, I started renovating.

People were screaming. Between one blow and another on the wall, I suddenly realized that people were screaming outside, not far from my house. I went outside. Near the intersection, thirty meters away, two people were lying on the road, and a woman was running toward me, yelling, and a man in a green woolen hat was chasing her. When there was maybe ten meters between us, he caught up with her and grabbed her by the hair. Suddenly, I saw the tip of a knife sticking out of the front of her neck. And blood, gallons of blood. She fell to her knees, the man twisted her arm behind her back, and the blade just disappeared. She was lying on the sidewalk now. And the guy with the knife was looking at me, moving slightly toward me, but slowly. I wanted to run away, but my feet just wouldn't budge. He kept coming closer, taking little, hesitant steps as if we were kids playing tag. And the whole time, I kept saying to myself, "Something's not right here. Why's he walking so slowly? I mean, he ran after that woman like a madman. Here I am in my slippers and he's holding a knife twenty centimeters long. What's he afraid of? Why doesn't he come up and stab me?" And then I saw him step off the sidewalk onto the road, trying to walk around me very, very slowly. I watched him, half aware of the sledgehammer in my hand, a five-kilo sledgehammer. I took a step toward him and whacked him on the head.

He wasn't moving. I sat down on the sidewalk. The grocery

guy came over with a Coke. I put my hand in the pocket of my sweatpants to pay him. He grabbed it and wouldn't let me take out the money. "Forget it," he said. "It's on me."

"Come on, Gaby," I said, "let me pay." But he insisted and wouldn't let go of my hand. "So put it on my bill," I said, backing down. I was thirsty and wanted to get things settled before I started drinking, while I was still in a bargaining position.

"Okay, okay," he said, "I'll put it on your bill."

The photographers got there first, even before the police. On motorcycles, two on a Honda 600F and one on a Harley. With their long hair and tattoos, they looked just like Hells Angels. "Would you hold the hammer like this, like you're threatening him, for a picture?" the guy with the Harley asked me. I said no. "Are you sure? It would be much stronger, in terms of visuals."

"Fuck the visuals," Gaby said. "Want something real? Get him in front of my store."

After that, the police came, then the newspaper reporters. All reporters are whores.

They came from all the papers. I wouldn't talk to them. They came from TV and from radio too. I didn't even tell them no, I just held up my hand and turned away. The TV people went over to Gaby and almost everybody else followed them, except the guy from *Ma'ariv*, who wouldn't get off my back.

"Hey you, four-eyes," I yelled to one of the newspaper reporters who was trying to shove his tape recorder down some police detective's throat. "Come here." The guy with the glasses left the policeman midsentence and rushed over. "You're from *Yediot*?" I asked.

"Yeah, I am," he panted, trying to turn the tape recorder on.

"Hey, how come you'll talk to him and not me?" said the nudnik from *Ma'ariv*.

"Because I feel like it, okay?" I was losing my patience. "Because your paper's shit. What difference does it make why? Please. Leave me alone."

I gestured for the guy with the glasses to follow me to the edge of the crowd, but the *Ma'ariv* guy was like glue. "It's because of their circulation," he said in a hurt voice. "It's just because of their circulation, you egomaniac. You wanna play it big-time, eh? So all your buddies can see what a hero you are? You macho shitwad, you murderer, you make me puke." He spat and left.

"Okay," the guy with the glasses said, "first of all I want to ask you—"

"First of all, you listen," I said. I took the tape recorder out of his hand and pressed Stop. "Go to your editor now and tell him I'm ready to give you an exclusive. An exclusive, got that? I won't talk to TV, or cable, or *Ma'ariv*. *I won't talk to my grandmother*. But only if—"

"We don't pay," said the guy with the glasses. "It's a matter of principle. We never pay for access."

"Listen to me for a second, you moron," I said. Now I was pissed. "I don't want your money. I just want to pick the interviewer. Understand what I'm saying? Tell him I'm ready to be interviewed, but only by Dafna Brosh."

"Brosh," said Glasses, scratching his head. "The new girl? She isn't exactly the sharpest knife in the drawer."

"She does the interview. Tell him."

"Excuse me," Glasses said, "I know this has nothing to do

with it, but did you happen to read my exposé on the circumcisers' cartel?"

"Dafna Brosh," I repeated and left him there.

To get to my apartment now, I had to walk through a huge circle of people who were standing around Gaby. They were shouting and screaming, and he was standing there in the middle, waving his hands. It looked like he was having a pretty good time. Two soldiers from the army radio station with mikes in their hands had come a little late and were trying to push their way into the circle but couldn't. One of them, the taller one, got an elbow in his face from the cameraman of one of the foreign networks. He started bleeding from the nose, his eyes welled up, and tears came streaming down. I decided to head in the other direction and get to my building through a parallel street. "Egomaniac!" the *Ma'ariv* guy yelled at my back.

She came. I knew she would. In a black miniskirt. She'd bobbed her hair. "Want some coffee?" I asked, trying to sound calm. "Should I put on the kettle?" She shook her head, sat down at the table, and took a mini–tape recorder out of her bag. There were large pieces of plaster scattered all over the table. With the half-knocked-down wall in the middle of the room, the place looked like a bomb site. "Sure?" I asked. "I'll put on the kettle."

The head shaking got sharper, more nervous. "An interview," she said, and the words came out as if she were choking, "I came for an interview." She put the tape recorder on the table.

INTERVIEW A

—Why?

—Am I allowed to ask exactly why you left me?

—Don't shrug your shoulders. Answer me. The least I deserve is an answer.

I don't want to hurt you. Definitely not now. There's no point in it.

—Hurt me, damn you, hurt me. It can't be worse than what you already did.

Because you're a nobody, okay? Because you're a nobody. Because you don't want anything. Nothing. Don't want to know anything, don't want to succeed at anything, don't want to be anything. Just to sit on your ass and say how good we have it together. Good is doing things, trying to achieve something, but you? You don't even know how to dream. You're not a person, you're nothing. The only thing you're capable of doing is sitting on that balcony with your arms around me, saying, "I love you, I love you, I love you." I'm not a teddy bear, you know? I'm not a Barbie. And unlike you, I have slightly bigger ambitions than sleeping in.

—Do you still love me?

—Do you love me a little?

—Did you ever love me?

—Hey, cut it out, don't cry. I'm stopping. I stopped. Look. Go ahead and ask your questions.

INTERVIEW B

—What were you doing on the street at the time of the incident?

Nothing.

—Were you on your way somewhere?

No. I wasn't on my way anywhere. I just heard yelling, so I went outside to see.

—And the hammer?

I whacked him on the head with it. God, when I try to remember that, it seems really distant, like something in a movie.

—Yes, but why did you have a hammer in your hand?

Because of the renovations. I'm knocking down the wall between the living room and the bedroom.

—Did you get a good look at him before it happened? Could you see his face?

Yes, his face was kind of chubby. He had these big brown eyes, like yours. And he pursed his lips, like something was wrong. Like he was constipated, in pain.

—What passed through your mind when you whacked him with the hammer?

Nothing.

—Don't say nothing. You thought something.

Nothing. Absolutely nothing.

—I talked to Gaby from the grocery. He told me that the Arab didn't get anywhere near you, that he was afraid when he saw you with the hammer, that he tried to walk around you, to get away. But you still smashed his skull. You could've waited, you know, you could've just stood there and he would've gone away. At least that's what the Eli I knew would've done. I was thinking of you.

We heard the sound of a motorcycle outside. "That's the photographer," she said. "His name's Eli too."

"What kind of bike does he ride?" I asked.

"Since when do I know anything about motorcycles?" she said, laughing.

"Just asking. I thought you might know."

"An FZR 1000. He has a Yamaha FZR 1000, the one you wished for."

"You know, if I hadn't told you then, I'd have one too."

"I know," she said and smiled. "I'm sorry."

PAINTING

Say someone agrees to paint you a painting. Any painting, nothing specific. You let him have your apartment for a month and in return he'll paint you a painting. You don't sign a contract or anything, but still it's a transaction like any other. Objectively speaking, everybody wins. You take advantage of his enormous talent as a painter, and he takes advantage of your oft-remarked talent for disappearing from the country for weeks at a time—to Thailand, to Japan, or in this case, to a good, solid, respectable destination, like France, for instance.

Know what? Make it Paris.

It remains to be determined whether the transaction is fair. It's legal, that's for sure, because there's mutual consent. But is it fair? To be honest, it's hard to say. You're sitting there, on the Champs-Elysées, sipping at a demitasse of espresso, while he has to paint away at your painting like a slave. On the other hand, the rent he'd have to pay for a place like yours, if he rented it for a month, would be much higher than the best price he could get for any of his paintings. Furthermore, the guy is shitting in your toilet, sleeping in your bed, covering himself with your blanket.

Not just him, maybe all sorts of other people too, people he brings home—you haven't got a clue. As for you, meanwhile, you're holed up in some tacky French hotel with a snotty concierge who can't understand English. When all is said and done, the Champs-Elysées is nothing to write home about, with the beating-down July sun frying your brains and a million Japanese tourists. God knows how you'll get through the month. A hypothetical God, of course, because none of this actually happens.

Now say two weeks in, you suddenly have to go home. Your wallet's been stolen, or maybe you only think it's been stolen when what really happened is you lost it. It fell out of your pocket, you dropped it—whatever. You're out of money, and you're going home. The agreement stipulated one month. Thus the question arises whether you have the right to return to your old apartment ahead of time. On the face of it, you do. But think again. Try to picture it the other way around. Suppose the other party to the transaction had lost his painting supplies. No, that's not a good analogy. Say he'd lost his talent. Would it be fair of you to demand that he finish the painting? But the analogy, in this case, falls apart, because talent is such an elusive commodity, one you don't exactly come across every day, whereas an apartment is a piece of property that's registered at the Housing Ministry, and French money is something you can easily get from your parents. At any rate, you're back, and you're both in the apartment, you in one bedroom and the other party in the other. At night you sometimes meet outside the bathroom.

The other party has a compelling face and a sexy body. Let's say you find it extremely attractive. But now you're sweating.

Know what? Let me make this easy on you: Say the other party
is a girl. A girl with a very attractive face and a body that turns
you on. Here, let me open a window.

Better?

The other party is prettier. Prettier than her paintings. Because pretty is what she is all the time, whereas painting is what
she does only when she isn't sleeping or eating or fucking men
you don't know on sheets you got from your parents for your
birthday. Know what? She uses her own sheets. But you know
the men. No, I won't say who, but a few of them are men you
know very well.

So, where were we? Right: the Champs-Elysées. You threw your
wallet somewhere and went home. The two of you have worked
it out. Each of you has a room. Except that, in this particular
case, your room is the one she gets. And the painting? Maybe
she doesn't fucking feel like it. Or maybe she does. It doesn't
seem right to ask. But all those men who keep coming and going
in the middle of the night, they make her scream. And you, to
you it seems very inconsiderate. Because just say you had been
able to fall asleep at night, it's not exactly as if you could have
slept through it. Anyway, what's the deal? Men you know, and I
won't say who, have her screaming in the middle of the night,
and then in the morning she hasn't got the energy to paint you
the painting that, according to contract, she has a legal and
moral obligation to deliver.

It's clear enough as far as you're concerned, but what are
you going to say? Get some sleep so you have energy to paint

me my painting? You'll never have the guts, especially not when you came back two weeks ahead of schedule. Besides, maybe she is working on it, working from models, from men you know. Like your big brother, for instance. In the middle of the night. And when he won't hold still, she screams at him. It's frustrating work. What is she painting? You really ought to find out. It has occurred to you that the painting itself may go a long way toward elucidating her feelings for you. Could she in fact be in love with you? Could this whole apartment transaction be a ruse for getting closer to you? Either way, would you mind letting go of your brother's throat? He's turning slightly blue.

Where were we? Something to do with blue. Well, in the end it turns out she was making you a painting of the sea. No, the sky. Ah, sorry, now you've strangled your brother. Ah yes, we were just saying how much you can learn about a person's character from a painting.

YORDAN

Even before he finished punching the secret code into the pad on his wall safe, Yordan felt something was wrong. A voice in the back of his mind said, "Run, Yordan, while you still can." But twelve long years with the Mossad had taught him to treat his sixth sense as skeptically as he treated the other five. And this time, his senses didn't disappoint him. The safe was empty. The three "deleted" files and his suede bag with the snaps were gone. For the first time since they killed his parents right before his eyes, Yordan permitted himself to blanch. "Don't panic," the voice in the back of his mind ordered him. "Think, think, think." Who could think with all that nagging? "No one knew the combination except my wife, Yemima," Yordan told himself, trying to narrow down the list of potential suspects, "and I killed her in November, after that saccharin-in-the-coffee fiasco." He stood in front of the empty safe completely at a loss. He was being punished now for the mistake he made in November when he left himself with a blank list of suspects. Or had he forgotten someone? Yordan remembered what Halamish taught him in basic training (before he was exposed as a mole for the

Khmer Rouge): "Trust no one, not even yourself." Suddenly it was clear. "I stole the files," he whispered to himself unbelievingly. "It all fits: I knew the combination, I had the opportunity. And who besides me had a reason to steal the suede bag with the snaps?" After the initial shock, Yordan resolved to act, and fast. He surprised himself from behind, overcame himself easily, and tied himself to a chair. "Who sent you?" he yelled furiously at himself. "Talk, asshole." "Hey, have you lost your mind?" he replied in confusion. "This is me, I mean, you, Yordan. Untie me." "Shut up, traitor," Yordan said and slapped himself. "Me, a traitor?" he said, surprised. "Yordan, are you crazy? You've known me since forever. You know I'd never betray the homeland." Yordan pretended to be convinced and untied himself. *"Tfadal,"* he said, handing himself a cigarette. *"Shukran,"* he said, thanking himself. "Aha! Now I've got you, you Arab son of a bitch," Yordan said excitedly. "Come on, is that any way to talk about Mama?" he replied, feigning innocence. "Cut the Mama shit, mole. If you're not a spy, why'd you answer me in Arabic?" "Because you asked in Arabic, dipshit. We learned Arabic together in basic training," Yordan said to himself, his feelings hurt, sincerity in his voice. "Trust him, he's telling the truth," the voice in the back of his mind whispered with a slight Russian accent. "After all, he is you. You have to trust him." "I have no duty but to sacrifice my life for my country," Yordan said to himself. "Besides . . . Hey, wait a minute, what's with that slight Russian accent?" He plunged his hand into the back of his mind and pulled out a dwarf in a Cossack hat.

While Yordan was driving the handcuffed midget to be interrogated at headquarters, the little man volunteered some information. "Look," he said, "ever since glasnost, there's been no work. All KGB guys are dying of boredom. So we decided to, how do you people say it, to pull a leg. We searched our files for an agent with the lowest IQ in the world and we—" Yordan didn't listen to the rest. He pulled out the car lighter, shoved the Soviet dwarf in the hole, reinserted the lighter, and pushed till he felt the click. Eight seconds later, the dwarf stopped screaming. Yordan made a U-turn and went home. "So maybe I was a little weak when they tested us on the shapes," he said to himself. "But the lowest IQ in the world? You know," he said to himself with false bonhomie, "I once knew a Georgian agent who could hardly count to three . . ." He smiled irresistibly into the mirror.

Deep down, he still didn't trust him.

VACUUM SEAL

The sergeant took Alon's vacuum-sealed bandage and pushed it into the pail. Air bubbles rose to the surface. The sergeant ignored them and went on pressing the bandage down to the bottom, smirking. Alon couldn't help feeling that the sergeant was trying to drown his bandage, his personal bandage, for no reason whatsoever.

The stream of bubbles stopped. The sergeant took his hand out of the pail and gave the wet corpse a look of contempt. "Is this what you call a vacuum seal, Schreiber? There's a hole in this seal that's as big as a cunt." The sergeant moved closer, till their faces were practically touching, and said in a loud whisper: "But I'm sorry, Schreiber. Have you ever once seen a girl's cunt?"

Alon had once seen a girl's cunt. Many times, in fact, although he couldn't find any connection between her naked and loving body and the sergeant's word.

"I asked you a question, Schreiber." Alon felt as if the sergeant had invaded his brain and was undressing her against her will, against his will. He wouldn't let him destroy that, too. He wouldn't.

"I can't hear you, Schreiber."

"No, sir."

"Never mind, it isn't your fault you were born a loser. Why don't you ask your mother nicely? Maybe she'll show you the hole you came out of. Lugassi, I wouldn't laugh if I had a face like yours."

The sergeant turned toward Alon. There was a menacing look in his eyes. "Am I imagining things, Schreiber, or are you crying?"

"No, sir."

"Schreiber, you're a piss-poor excuse for a human being, a piss-poor excuse for a soldier, and a piss-poor excuse for a vacuum sealer." By now the sergeant was screaming, spraying droplets of spit in Alon's face. The droplets stung, like an all-consuming acid. "I can't make a man out of you. Even God almighty couldn't do that. But I can make a soldier out of you. Tomorrow morning, I expect to see every single one of your shorts and undershirts vacuum-sealed. One by one. And they'd better be done properly this time. And you know why, Schreiber?" The sergeant's voice rose even higher. "Because good vacuum sealing is an inseparable part of being a good soldier. I bet you're smiling, Bugamilsky." The sergeant turned to face Bugamilsky with a nervous jerk. "It'd take a cherry retard like you to smile when I'm explaining about vacuum sealing. I'd like to see you smile after you cross the Zahrani with your pants full of Arab shit and filth. And then, when you want to change into a clean pair of pants and some clean, dry underwear"—the sergeant moved over toward Bugamilsky's bed, opened the rucksack, and registered a look of mock surprise—"you'll discover it's on account of your lousy vacuum seal that they're sopping wet too. I bet you'll be laughing then too, dickbrain, when you try to keep going with a ton of filth in your shorts, like some baby that made in his pants.

"Bugamilsky didn't take his vacuum sealing seriously, which is why he's going to do two extra hours of guard duty tonight. Private, write that down. Anyone else here too smart to bother with vacuum sealing?" The sergeant scanned the platoon.

Alon did take it seriously. Vacuum sealing was his only chance.

That night, Alon vacuum-sealed his clothes. The more he sealed, he could tell, the more he got the hang of it, and he couldn't help feeling proud as he studied his last vacuum-sealed undershirt. He was ready.

He closed his eyes softly and started to vacuum-seal himself.

During roll call, the sergeant was more short-tempered than ever, handing out punishments right, left, and center. When he got to Alon, he grabbed him by his shirt, leaned over, and shouted the same sentence in his ear over and over again. Alon listened to the drops of spittle shattering against the vacuum seal. Their frenzied rhythm reminded him of raindrops banging helplessly against a taut plastic awning. Not a single droplet hit him.

That night, he had to crawl for fifty minutes, shouting "I'm a snake, I'm a liar," because he'd assured the sergeant that his weapon was clean and the sergeant had found some oil in the assembly.

When Schreiber rose to his feet, he was pleased to discover that not a single drop of dirt had stuck to him. The vacuum seal had done its job.

Only once did Schreiber doubt the perfection of the seal. It was his Saturday off, two weeks before the end of basic training. She said that the army had changed him, had made him different, that he was avoiding her kisses, pulling away when she touched him. How could he tell her about the synthetic taste in his mouth, the fake, sticky feel of her body, the suffocation? For a moment he thought he'd heard the sound of air rushing through some hidden hole in the transparent seal. But it was just the murmur of the door closing behind her. He wanted to cry, but there were no tears in his eyes. Anyway, what's the point of a transparent vacuum seal if you get yourself wet inside?

He looked at himself in the mirror, at his shiny dog tag, at his neatly starched service dress, at the razor in his right hand. He drew the razor closer to the clearly visible artery in his neck. "Basic training is over," he whispered. "Time to undo the seal."

THE GIRL ON
THE FRIDGE

ALONE

He told her that he once had a girlfriend who liked to be
alone. And that was very sad, because they were a couple,
and *couple*, by definition, means "together." But mostly she
preferred to be alone. So once he asked her, "Why? Is it me?"

And she said, "No, it has nothing to do with you, it's me, it
has to do with my childhood."

He really didn't get it, the childhood thing, so he tried to find
an analogy in his own childhood, but he came up empty. The
more he thought about it, the more his childhood seemed like
a cavity in somebody else's tooth—unhealthy, but no big deal,
at least not to him. And that girl, who liked to be alone, kept
hiding from him, and all because of her childhood. It pissed
him off. Finally, he told her, "Either you explain it to me or we
stop being a couple." She said okay, and they stopped being a
couple.

OGETTE IS SYMPATHETIC

"That's very sad," Ogette said. "Sad and, at the same time, moving."

"Thanks," Nahum said and took a sip of his juice.

Ogette saw there were tears in his eyes, and she didn't want to upset him, but in the end she couldn't resist. "So to this day," she asked, "you don't know what it was in her childhood that made her leave you?"

"She didn't leave me," Nahum corrected her. "We broke up."

"Broke up, whatever," Ogette said.

"It's not 'whatever,' " Nahum insisted, "it's my life. For me, at least, those are significant distinctions."

"And to this day, you don't know what event in her childhood started all this?" Ogette continued.

"It wasn't any event," Nahum corrected her again. "No one started anything—no one but you here now." And after a short silence, he added, "Yeah, it had something to do with the refrigerator."

NOT NAHUM'S

When Nahum's girlfriend was little, her parents had no patience for her because she was little and full of energy, and they were already old and worn-out. Nahum's girlfriend tried to play with them, to talk to them, but that only annoyed them more. They didn't have the strength. They didn't even have enough strength to tell her to shut her mouth. So instead, they used to hoist her up, sit her on the refrigerator, and go to work. Or wherever they had to go. The refrigerator was very high, and Nahum's girl-friend couldn't get down. And so it happened that she spent most of her childhood on top of the refrigerator. It was a very happy childhood. While other people got the crap beaten out of them by their big brothers, Nahum's girlfriend sat on the edge of the fridge, sang to herself, and drew little pictures in the layer of dust around her. The view from up there was very beautiful, and her bottom was nice and warm. Now that she was older, she missed that time, that alone time, very much. Nahum under-stood how sad it made her, and once he even tried to fuck her on top of the refrigerator, but that didn't work.

"That's an awfully beautiful story," Ogette whispered, brush-ing Nahum's hand with hers.

"Yes," Nahum mumbled, pulling his arm back. "An awfully beautiful story, but it isn't mine."

WORLD CHAMPION

In honor of my dad's fiftieth, I brought him a gold-plated navel cleaner with FOR THE MAN WHO HAS EVERYTHING inscribed across the handle. It was a toss-up between that and *Axis of Evil—Axis of Hope*. I spent a long time going back and forth. My dad was in a good mood all evening. He was the life of the party. He showed everyone how he brushed his navel clean, and he trumpeted like a happy elephant. My mom kept telling him, "Come on, Menachem, give it a rest." But he didn't.

In honor of my dad's fiftieth, the tenant who lives in the up-stairs apartment decided he wasn't leaving, even though his lease was up. "Look, Mr. Fullman," he said, hunched over a dis-mantled Marantz amp, like a butcher. "In February I'm off to New York to open a stereo lab with my brother-in-law, and I'm not about to move all my shit out just to move it again in two months." And when my dad told him the lease was up in De-cember, Electronics Man went right on working as if nothing had happened and said in the tone you use to shake off one of those door-to-door guys asking for donations to a worthy cause, "Lease-shmease, I'm staying. You don't like it? Then sue me," and stabbed his screwdriver all the way through the amplifier's guts.

In honor of my dad's fiftieth, I went with him to see his lawyer, and the lawyer said our hands were tied. "Settle," he suggested, rummaging through his drawer in a desperate search for something. "Try to get another three, four hundred out of him, and leave it at that. A lawsuit, you'll get an ulcer, and after two years of running around that may be all you get."

In honor of my dad's fiftieth, I asked him why we don't just go into Electronics Man's apartment at night and change the lock and dump all his stuff in the front yard. And my dad said that was illegal, and I shouldn't even think about it. I asked if it was because he was afraid, and he said no, just realistic. "What's the point?" he asked and rubbed his bald spot. "You tell me, what is the point? Over a couple of months? Forget it, it's not worth the effort."

In honor of my dad's fiftieth, I thought back about what he'd been like when I was a kid. A towering man who worked for the city. He took me places. He'd carry me piggyback. I'd yell "Giddyup," and he'd run up and down the stairs, with me on his back like a lunatic. Back then he wasn't realistic. He was world champion.

In honor of my dad's fiftieth, I stood on the landing and took a good look. He was bald, he had a little potbelly, he hated his wife, who was my mom. People kept stepping on him and he'd tell himself it wasn't worth the effort. I thought of the asshole tenant stabbing amplifiers up there in the apartment that had belonged to my grandfather who was dead, and just knowing that my dad won't do a thing, because he's tired, because he hasn't got the balls. Because even his son, who's only twenty-three, won't do a thing.

In honor of my dad's fiftieth, I thought about life for a second. About how it spits in your face. About how you're always letting assholes have their way because they're not worth the effort. I thought about myself, about my girlfriend, Tali, who I don't really love, about the bald spot hiding under my hairline, about the inertia that somehow always keeps me from telling a girl I don't know on the bus that she's really pretty, from getting off when she does and buying her flowers. My dad had gone back inside, and I was left on the landing by myself. The light clicked off and I didn't even go turn it back on. I felt as if I was choking. I felt like a Coke that's gone flat. I thought about my kids, who'd go scurrying like mice through an underground mall just to bring me back a copy of *Axis of Evil—Axis of Hope*.

In honor of my dad's fiftieth, I whacked his tenant across the face with a wrench. "You broke my nose," Shlomi whimpered, writhing on the floor. "You broke my nose."

"Nose-shnose." I lifted the Phillips screwdriver off his workbench. "You don't like it? Then sue me." I thought about my dad, who must be sitting in the bedroom now, cleaning his navel with a brush with a gold-plated handle. It pissed me off. It enraged me. I put the screwdriver down and gave him a kick in the head for good measure.

NO POLITICS

In the corner of the balcony next to the stained picture of Demis Roussos sat a scary bald guy no one knew, eating olives and trying to hit the garbage cans in the yard with the pits. "In my café, you can talk about anything but politics," the Romanian reminded the table near the door. "Gossip, talk about sports, even sex if you want to, just no politics. It ruins everyone's appetite." They say that once, when the café had just opened—the British were still here—some Revisionist called Ben-Gurion a "midget" and there was such a brawl that not a single table was left standing.

"Pussy kills my appetite, too," Davidoff muttered under his breath. "Besides, it's not as if anyone comes here to eat." But everyone respected the Romanian, so they started talking about the mosquitoes, which bit everyone but Mitzenmacher's wife; even they were afraid to get close to her. The bald guy in the corner coughed once, dramatically. And when they all looked over, he started to speak:

"All the parties are swindlers and cowards, believe me," he said in a booming voice. "Take the religious parties, for instance.

They turn the country upside down, then laugh in our faces." The café was suddenly silent, and from behind the espresso machine came the sound of breaking glass.

Davidoff chuckled with pleasure and said, "The Romanian broke another glass."

"Wait a minute. Am I right or not?" the bald guy continued in a provocative voice, waving the newspaper he'd been hiding under his napkin as proof. "There's a story in today's paper about a million dollars they gave to some yeshiva that didn't even exist—it was, you know, 'fictitious'—while other people break their asses out in the sticks and go to live in tents—"

"Sir, it is one of the unwritten laws of this institution that there will be no discussion of—" Mitzenmacher said, in the style he'd developed back when he worked at the Ministry of the Interior.

"Calm down, Mitzi," said Davidoff. "Let the man express himself." Davidoff put a hand on Mitzi's shoulder, hiding a malicious smile.

The bald guy waved a thank-you to Davidoff, ate another olive, threw the pit from the balcony, and went on talking. "And it's not just the religious ones, it's all of them. A corrupt government, that's what we have . . ." The Romanian appeared from behind the counter and starting walking toward the bald guy, gripping the tables as he moved, his forehead red and sweaty, his scrawny arms looking hairier than usual. ". . . Believe me, if it was up to me, I'd kill all hundred and sixty Knesset members," the bald guy continued in his aggressive voice.

"But there's only a hundred and twenty," Davidoff said, egging him on.

"First we'll kill forty," the bald guy said and snickered, "and when they put new ones in their place, we knock off all hundred and twenty at once."

"I am asking you to leave the café right now," the Romanian ordered in a broken voice, his long face covered with dark stubble.

"Hey, what's with you, old man?" the bald guy hissed and popped another olive in his mouth. "We're talking a little politics here, so what? We live in this country, right? So we're not allowed to say a word?"

"I demand that you leave right now," the Romanian rasped, leaning on a chair, the beads of sweat dripping from his bushy eyebrows into his thick beard.

"Would it be such a tragedy . . . ," Mitzenmacher muttered, trying to get up from his chair again.

"Come on, Mitzi, sit down and eat your ice-cream cake before it turns into milk-shake cake," Davidoff ordered, and Mitzenmacher fell back into his seat.

"The problem with this country is that we have people like you," the bald guy continued, shoving the olive pit into the Romanian's apron pocket, "who got used to keeping quiet and eating the shit. Believe me, if you'd opened your traps thirty years ago, those gangsters wouldn't be sitting in the Knesset today." The back of the chair broke under the Romanian's weight, but he remained standing, a quiet growl issuing from his drooling mouth. "All that stealing started a long time ago. Anyone who knows a little history will tell you that Ben-Gurion . . ."

"Uh-oh," Davidoff said. This was, ostensibly, a warning.

The Romanian gave a bloodcurdling roar, jumped through

the air, and ripped out a piece of the bald guy's shoulder with his canines. It was over in seconds.

"Believe me," said Davidoff with a chuckle, "I haven't seen the Romanian this worked up since Passover, two years ago, when a guy started talking about the embargo."

"You should be ashamed of yourself." Mitzenmacher rebuked him and went to help the Romanian, who was sitting on the floor, hiding his face in his blood-soaked apron and whimpering.

"I don't know what came over me, I turned into a real animal," he wailed. "It's from Transylvania. Back there they never stopped with the politics . . ." He started to cry.

"There, there," said Mitzenmacher, stroking his head, trying to console him. "And you," he called to Davidoff, who was sharing his thoughts with the others at his table, "bury this poor bastard in the yard."

"But I haven't finished my coffee," said Davidoff, trying to weasel out of it. "Let someone else do it."

Mitzenmacher glared and handed him a shovel.

"Okay, okay," Davidoff said, rising. "But I better not get any blood on my Lacoste shirt. I only just got it last week." And with that he rolled up his sleeves.

THE REAL WINNER OF THE PRELIMINARY GAMES

To Eyal

They used to talk a lot about life, about this and that: yes I'm happy, no I'm not happy, I miss that girl, I want that job, I'm looking for a challenge. Most of the time, they lied. Not on purpose, it just happened, and after a while they both started getting tired of it. So they stopped that, and moved on to other things, like the stock market, or sports. Then Uzi came up with the idea of the four-beer test. It was simple: every three weeks they'd go into a bar and they'd each drink four pints. The first they'd polish off without a word. After the second one they'd talk about how they felt, the same after numbers three and four. They always left a big tip. Sometimes they'd throw up, but the owners got used to it. Then Eitan went off to reserve duty for a month, and after that Uzi had this big project at work, so they wound up not meeting for six weeks. In those six weeks, Eitan grew a really cool little hippie-style beard and Uzi quit smoking three different times.

"Today we'll have to order eight beers," Uzi said as they went into the bar, "to make up for lost time."

Eitan smiled. They weren't big drinkers, and even four pints was much too much. The TV was on over the bar, but without the sound. They were showing the highlights from the first heats in the Commonwealth Games.

"Check out the British dude, how happy he looks." Uzi laughed and pointed at a scrawny figure jumping up and down on the screen. "What's he getting so worked up about? All he did was come in first in his heat in the pre-prelims of some godforsaken race. It's like the pre-Eurovision of track and field. The way he's jumping around you'd think he'd won three Olympic medals—platinum."

"When it comes to long distance, the Europeans don't stand a chance, not in the Olympics," Eitan said. "The Africans are destroying them. The Commonwealth's all they've got."

"No shit," Uzi persisted, "but just because he hasn't got a chance of placing at the Olympics, is that any reason to be jumping for joy? Besides, he hasn't actually won anything yet, it's only the heats."

They downed the first beer, then the second. Uzi asked Eitan about his stint in the reserves. Eitan said it had been okay. Eitan asked him how the project had gone.

"Okay," Uzi said. "Really. Okay. But for the past couple of months I've been feeling, I don't know, kind of down. The spark just isn't there. Not when I go in, not while I'm working, not when I go home at night. No spark. You know?"

They drank their third and Eitan said that was how it was, everyone feels that way sometimes. He could hold his liquor much better than Uzi. Whenever anyone threw up, it tended to be Uzi. According to the rules, Uzi was supposed to say something too, but he didn't. He just bummed a cigarette off the waitress, lit up, and stared at the screen. It was some variety show with Dolly Parton and Kenny Rogers. Eitan kidded him about how he could ask the barman to turn up the volume. Uzi didn't even answer.

"I thought you said the acupuncture did you some good," Eitan said, looking at Uzi, who'd smoked his cigarette all the way down and was trying not to burn his fingers on the butt.

"That Dr. Weiss is a charlatan," said Uzi. "Acupuncture doesn't do shit."

The waitress smoked filterless. Uzi took one long final drag and it vanished like magic. He didn't even have to put it out or anything, there was simply nothing left. They drank the fourth pint. Eitan barely managed to finish, he was feeling sick as hell. Uzi was actually looking cool and asked the waitress for another cigarette.

"Tell you something," Uzi said once that cigarette had vanished too, "I've had it."

"With the cigarettes?"

"With everything." Uzi pushed down hard on the ashtray, like he was trying to extinguish his finger too. "With everything. None of it means anything, none of it. You know how it feels when you're someplace and you ask yourself, Why am I here? That's how it is with me all the time. I can't wait to leave. To go from wherever I am to some other place. It never ends. I swear, I'd have killed myself a long time ago if I wasn't such a pussy."

"Cut it out," Eitan tried. "That isn't you talking, it's the beer. Tomorrow you're going to wake up feeling like hell and you'll tell yourself you were talking some serious bullshit. Then you'll decide to quit smoking."

Uzi didn't laugh. "I know," he muttered. "I know it's the beer. Tomorrow I'll sound different. I thought that was the whole point."

They took a cab home. The first stop was Uzi's.

"Take care of yourself, okay?" Eitan said and gave him a hug before he got out of the cab. "Don't do anything retarded."

"Don't worry." Uzi smiled. "I'm not going to kill myself or anything. I don't have the balls. If I did, I'd have done it a long time ago."

Next, the cab dropped Eitan at his place, and he went upstairs. He had a gun in the drawer. He'd bought it with sporting-goods coupons he'd received when he was an officer. Not that he was trigger-happy or anything, but it was either that or signing for an M16 every time he went on leave. Eitan took the gun out of his underwear drawer and cocked it. He held it up to his chin. Someone had told him once that if you shoot from underneath, it wipes out your brain stem. When you shoot at the temple, the slug could go right through and you'd wind up a vegetable. He released the safety.

"If I want to, I can shoot," he said out loud. He ordered his brain to pull the trigger. His finger obeyed, but stopped halfway. He could do it, he wasn't scared. He just had to make sure he wanted to. He thought about it for a few seconds. Maybe in the general scheme of things he couldn't find any meaning to life, but on a smaller scale it was okay. Not always, but a lot of the time. He wanted to live, he really did. That's all there was to it. Eitan gave his finger another order to make sure he wasn't kidding himself. It still seemed prepared to do whatever he wanted. He put the gun on half cock and pushed the safety back in. If not for those four beers, he'd never even have tried it. He would have made up an excuse, said it was just a dumb test, that it didn't mean anything. But like Uzi said, that was the whole point. He put the gun back in the drawer and went into the bathroom to puke. Then he washed his face and soaked his head in the sink. Before drying himself, he took a look in the mirror. A skinny guy, wet hair, a little pale, like that runner on TV. He wasn't jumping or yelling or anything, but he'd never felt this good.

CRAMPS

That night I dreamed that I was a forty-year-old woman and my husband was a retired colonel. He was running a community center in a poor neighborhood, and his social skills were shit. His workers hated him because he kept yelling at them. They complained that he treated them like they were in basic training. Every morning I'd make him an omelet, and for supper a veal cutlet with mashed potatoes. When he was in a decent mood, he'd say the food tasted good. He never offered to clear the table. Once a month or so, he'd bring home a bouquet of dead flowers that immigrant kids used to sell at the intersection where the lights were really slow.

That night I dreamed that I was a forty-year-old woman and that I was having cramps, and it's nighttime, and suddenly I realize I'm all out of tampons, and I try to wake my husband, who's a retired colonel, and ask him to go to the all-night pharmacy or to drive me there at least, because I don't have a driver's license, and even if I did, he still has an army car I'm not allowed to drive. I tell him it's an emergency, but he won't go, just keeps mumbling in his sleep, saying the meal was lousy, and that if the cooks thought they were getting furlough, they could just forget it, because this was the army and not some fucking summer camp. I stuffed in a folded Kleenex and tried lying on my back without breathing, to keep it from leaking. But my whole body hurt, and the blood was gushing out of me, sounding like a broken sewage pipe. It leaked over my hips, and my legs, and splashed over my stomach. And the tissue turned into a wad that stuck to my hair and my skin.

That night I dreamed that I was a forty-year-old woman and that I was disgusted with myself, with my life. With not having a driver's license, with not knowing English, with never having been abroad. The blood that had dripped all over me was beginning to harden, and it felt like a kind of curse. Like my period would never end.

That night I dreamed that I was a forty-year-old woman and that I fell asleep and dreamed I was a twenty-seven-year-old man who gets his wife pregnant, and then finishes medical school and forces her and the baby to join him when he goes to do his residency abroad. They suffer terribly. They don't know a word of English. They don't have any friends, and it's cold outside, and snowing. And then, one Sunday, I take them on a picnic and spread out the blanket on the lawn, and they put out the food they've brought. And after we finish eating, I take out a hunting rifle and I shoot them like dogs. The policemen come to my house. The finest detectives in the Bloomington police force try to make me confess. They put me in this room, they yell at me, they won't let me smoke, they won't let me go to the bathroom, but I don't crack. And my husband beside me in bed keeps yelling, "I don't give a goddamn how you did it before. Around here I'm the commander now!"

A NO-MAGICIAN
BIRTHDAY

In November '93, Dov Genichovsky announced the new municipal tax collection ordinance on national radio. My mother, who even at fifty-three was still a raving beauty, had begun to drag her feet across the floor. Her smile stayed the same, she felt the same when you hugged her, she still had plenty of strength in her arms, but now when she walked she shuffled her feet. If you looked hard at the X-rays, you could spot black worms drilling into her kidneys. My birthday was coming up. The date's very easy to remember: December 21, 12/21. I knew she'd be planning something special, like every other year.

The winter of '93 was probably the coldest winter of my life. I was living on my own, sleeping in sweats and socks, and every night, I'd make sure to tuck the top deep into my pants so if I turned in my sleep, my back wouldn't be exposed. The Channel Two project had just fallen through, the paper wouldn't give me a raise, and my ex-girlfriend was going around town telling everyone I was gay and impotent. I'd wake up in the middle of the night with my armpits reeking of decay. I'd call her, and as a precaution I'd put my hand over the receiver even when I was dialing—and when she'd answer I'd hang up. I was convinced I was getting back at her, big time.

We put off my birthday by a day, because on the evening of the twentieth the paper sent me to an observatory to bring back a thousand words about a meteor belt that traveled past us only every hundred years. I asked if I could write about the settler from Hebron who'd been hit in the head and turned into a vegetable, but they told me it wasn't my beat. My beat was human interest. Every week I had to come up with a human interest feature for pages 16–17 of the supplement, so that anyone who'd made it through the security-crime-finance-politics stories would get a bonus: a world convention of veterinarians, skateboard championship of the universe, something upbeat. I kept pushing for the settler who'd gotten whacked on the head with a brick. I identified with him. His project had fallen through, too. His prospects had dimmed. But my editor turned me down, again, so I headed for the Hadera Observatory with a photographer I'd never met. This photographer told me he'd been pissed off at the paper for the past month or so. He had in his possession the picture of a soldier who'd been murdered in the territories—a blood-and-gore shot of the guy's head skewered on a spike—and the editor was too pussy to print it. He'd said it was cheap.

"I wonder what he'd say about David fucking Lynch," said the photographer, taking it out on the stick shift of the rental. "Or Peckinpah—I guess he's 'cheap' too. The picture I shot of that Almakayess guy doesn't belong in a paper. It belongs in a fucking museum."

I tried to guess what my mother would be setting up for my birthday. The present would probably be a mini–cassette recorder. That was the thing I needed most, anyway. And for the occasion she'd bake me a carrot cake because it's my favorite. We'd sit around and chat, my brother would drive in especially from Raanana. My dad would tell me how proud he was of me, and he'd show me a scrapbook with all the stories I've written pasted on the black pages. I don't know why, but it made me think of my tenth birthday, how the whole class came, and my parents hired a magician.

The photographer and I reached the observatory. It was freezing, and I was supposed to be talking with all the meteor buffs who were hanging around there, getting copy. The people I met told me these weren't just meteors that move past us every one hundred years, but a group of meteors that passes by planet Earth once in seven centuries. My tape recorder wasn't working, so I had to take everything down in longhand.

"This is fucked up," the photographer griped. "People on the West Bank are slaughtering each other, and here I am shooting a bunch of shortsighted dorks in parkas jerking off on a telescope. Those moon rocks better come out good." Besides the cake, my mother would make the spaghetti I love, and carrot soup. And whenever she headed back toward the kitchen with that tired walk, I'd want to die.

The meteors came, the way they do every seven hundred years, and the photographer said it looked like shit and would look even shittier in the paper. If they were going to take so long coming around, he said, the least they could do was make it worth our while. And I kept thinking that if there was no magician, those meteors should come to our house instead. And burn everything down. My mother, my brother, the worms in her guts, me, with my fifteen hundred words for pages 16–17. That would make everyone happy. Even my ex-girlfriend would sleep easier at night. Like that birthday with the magician, when the coins kept spilling out of my brother's ears and mine. When my mother floated on air like a ballerina on the moon, when my father just smiled and said nothing.

THROUGH WALLS

She had this vague look in her eyes, half disappointed, half what's-the-difference. Like someone who realized he bought skim milk by mistake and doesn't have the energy to take it back. "It's really nice," she said, putting the cactus in a corner of the room. Then she said, "Look, Yoav, I don't know what you have in mind, it's just important to me that you know I'm living here with someone."

Once, I thought it was extremely important for my girlfriend to be pretty. It was essential that she be smart and we had to be in love and all that, but I really, really wanted her to be pretty, too. I was reading a lot of comic books in those days. My hero was The Vision. He could fly, he could walk through walls. He could kill you with a look. The Vision wasn't a person, he was an android. You couldn't tell from looking at him, he had a girlfriend and everything. He was special. He didn't look like anyone I'd ever met. He had a red face with a jewel in the middle of his forehead and a green suit. The Vision always wore green no matter what.

Sometimes I'd bump into her at parties. She'd come with her

boyfriend. He looked okay, but ordinary. She didn't look like anyone I'd ever met. When they stood together at a party, surrounded by dozens of people, you could tell just by looking who was the lead and who was the extra. She deserved better, and I knew it. I could have shaken her, I wanted to snatch her away. I didn't understand why I never said a word.

The Vision may have been made of synthetics, but he had lots of feelings. In one book he even cried. It was on the last page, and the caption read "Even an android can cry." He was big. He was a giant. He was the leader of the Avengers. Her boyfriend and I once peed next to each other in a campus bathroom, and his urine came out dark yellow. I wanted to kill him. For myself, but also because he defiled her with that ordinariness of his. I saw myself drowning him in the toilet, killing him with a death stare. But I didn't do that. I didn't do anything. He shook himself twice, put it in his pants, and zipped up. He didn't even flush. When he finished washing his hands, he put them under the dryer. I could have smashed his head against the mirror, the sink, the floor, a hundred places. He smiled at me, completely unafraid, and walked out.

I was mad at myself. I felt terrible. I knew the feeling would never end, like a headache that won't go away. I looked in the filthy mirror across from me. I was special, I didn't look like anyone I'd ever met. I could have shaken myself, I wanted to snatch myself away. I knew I deserved better. I didn't understand why I hadn't said a word.

Ronit got married in August. Her boyfriend became her husband. According to my parents, he's a very nice guy, but I knew. He won't go through walls for her. Neither will I. I did go through glass once. At a student demonstration. Two policemen threw me through a store window. A few years later, we met on the street. She had a baby. She asked me what the scar was from, then she started to cry. "God," she said. "What they did to your face." I gave the baby my death stare. It didn't work. Five seconds later he was crying too. "God, you were so beautiful," she said, wiping her face with a diaper. She never even noticed her baby screaming. Once, I'd have gone through walls for her.

QUANTA

On Yom Kippur Eve, the quanta went to ask Einstein for his forgiveness. "I'm not home," Einstein yelled at them from behind his locked door. On their way back, people swore loudly at them through the windows, and someone even threw a can. The quanta pretended not to care, but deep in their hearts they were really hurt. Nobody understands the quanta, everybody hates them.

"You parasites," people would shout at them as they walked down the road.

"Go serve in the army."

"We wanted to, actually," the quanta would try to explain, "but the army wouldn't take us because we're so tiny." Not that anyone listened. Nobody listens to the quanta when they try to defend themselves, but when they say something that can be interpreted negatively, well, then everyone's all ears. The quanta can make the most innocent statement, like "Look, there's a cat!" and right away they're saying on the news how the quanta were stirring up trouble and they rush off to interview Schrödinger. All in all, the media hated the quanta worse than anybody, because once the quanta had spoken at an IBM conference about how the very act of viewing had an effect on an event, and all the journalists thought the quanta were lobbying to keep them from covering the Intifada. The quanta could insist as much as they wanted that this wasn't at all what they meant and that they had no political agenda whatsoever, but nobody would believe them anyway. Everyone knew they were friends of the government's Chief Scientist.

Loads of people think the quanta are indifferent, that they have no feelings, but it simply isn't true. On Friday, after the program about the bombing of Hiroshima, they were interviewed in the studio in Jerusalem. They could barely talk. They just sat there facing the open mike and sniffling, and all the viewers at home, who didn't know the quanta very well, thought they were avoiding the question and didn't realize the quanta were crying. What's sad is that even if the quanta were to write dozens of letters to the editors of all the scientific journals in the world and prove beyond a doubt that when it came to the atom bomb they had simply been used, and that people had taken advantage of their naïveté, and that they'd never ever imagined it would end that way, it wouldn't do them any good, because nobody understands the quanta. The physicists least of all.

ONE HUNDRED PERCENT

I touch her hands, her face, her pussy, her shirt. And I say to her, "Roni, please. Take it off, for me." But she won't. So I back down and we start fooling around again, completely naked, almost. The tag on her shirt says the material is one hundred percent cotton. It's supposed to feel good, but it's scratchy. Nothing is one hundred percent, that's what she always says. Ninety-nine point nine, tops. And that's when you're lucky. And then she crosses her fingers for luck.

I hate that shirt. It's itchy on my face, it doesn't let me feel how warm her body is, or if she's sweating like me. And I say it again: "Roni, please." It comes out a quiet scream, like the sound of someone biting his cheek with his mouth closed. "I'm coming. Please take it off." She won't budge. She never does.

It's crazy. We've been together six months and I still haven't seen her naked. Six months, and my friends are still telling me not to make the next move. Six months of living together and they keep on telling me stories that all of them already know by heart. How she stood in front of the mirror and tried to cut her breasts off with a kitchen knife because she hated her body. How she was hospitalized, more than once. And they tell me those stories about her as if she were a stranger, while they're drinking our coffee from our mugs. They tell me not to get in over my head when we're already madly in love. It makes me want to strangle them, but I don't say anything. At most, I ask them to cut it out and I hate them silently. What can they tell me that I don't already know? What can they say that would make me love her even a tiny bit less?

I try to explain it to her. How it doesn't matter. How what we have is so strong that nothing can destroy it, then I cross my fingers for luck because she says so. How I know, how I've already been told, I know what's there and I couldn't care less. But it doesn't help. Nothing helps. She won't budge. The furthest we ever got was after a bottle of Chianti at a New Year's party, and even then, she only undid one button.

After the test comes back, she calls her girlfriend, who did it once, to find out about the procedure. She doesn't want an abortion, I can feel that. I don't want one either. That's what I tell her. I get down on my knees, like in the movies, and ask her to marry me: "Come on, babe," I say in my best Dean Martin voice. "Let's ring-a-ding-ding." She laughs; she says no. She asks if this is because of her being pregnant, but she knows it isn't. Five minutes later, she says okay, but on the condition that, if it's a boy, we call him Yotam. We shake on it. I try to get up, but my legs have fallen asleep.

That night, we get into bed. We kiss. We undress. Only the shirt stays on. She pushes me away. She unbuttons a button.

And another one, slowly, like a stripper, one hand holding the collar closed, the other undoing the next button down. After she's gone through them all, she looks at me, looks deep into my eyes. I'm gasping for breath. She lets the shirt fall open. And I see, I see what's underneath. Nothing could destroy what there is between us, nothing, that's what I always said. How could I ever have been so stupid?

NOT HUMAN BEINGS

D avidoff, the regiment commander's driver, was the first to see him. "Here comes trouble," he said, getting up from the empty ammo box he was sitting on.

"He's just a Border Police officer," said Stein, completely focused on the backgammon board.

"You know what that means," said Davidoff, still standing there and staring at the officer in the strange olive green uniform.

"No, I don't know," Stein muttered impatiently, "so how about sitting down already. It's your turn."

"It means they're going to move one of our guys over to them, 'personnel reinforcement' they call it. This isn't the first time."

"So they'll move someone over to them, big deal. Shoot the dice already, Davidoff."

"Maybe for you it's no big deal, but for the poor—"

"I swear, Davidoff, if you don't shoot the fucking dice, I'll go to the personnel officer right now and ask him to send *me*. Maybe with those guys, I'll at least be able to finish a game."

"You know, Stein," Davidoff said, ungluing his eyes from the Border Police officer, "sometimes you can be such an asshole. One day with them"—he pointed at the officer—"one day with them, and you'll sing a different tune. You never met guys like that, they'll eat you alive. Especially an Ashkenazi putz like you." Davidoff gave a dry laugh. "They'll have to scrape you off the bumper of their jeep."

"Fuck it, we're never going to get through this game today," Stein said, pissed off. He'd just stood up when Shaharabani, all sweaty, came over and said the personnel officer wanted to talk to him.

"Those Border Police pricks, they're a different army, they don't think like us at all. They're wild animals," the personnel officer said, digging around in his ear with his pen. "And that's exactly why I have to send them a good soldier who won't react to their provocations, not a hot-tempered one like Ackerman or Shaharabani who, best-case scenario, ends up in jail, worst-case in the hospital."

Stein packed his things and got into the jeep with the officer. He could've done without that compliment. "It's not so bad. Only a week," he thought, trying to cheer himself up. He could see Hamama's you-have-my-condolences face in the distance as they drove off.

"Okay, who's the prick that stole my commando knife?" asked the squat, hairy guy who was walking around the tent buck naked.

"Cool it, Zanzuri, I just took it for a second to cut the duct tape." A sweaty black soldier handed him a huge knife with a compass on the handle. Zanzuri snatched the knife and, in the same gesture, pressed it against the black guy's throat. "Shafik, you Bedouin asshole. You put your sweaty hands on my things one more time and I'll stick this knife up your black ass. You hear me?"

The officer who came into the tent ignored the incident. "Your bunk's over there," he said, pointing to the far end. "What did you say your name was?"

"Stein, Shmulik Stein," Stein mumbled.

"Your bunk's over there, Stein." He pointed to the same bed again. "Patrol in two hours, be ready."

Whenever he went out on patrol in one of those armored, rock-resistant jeeps, there were always riots. They couldn't drive down a single street without a brick flying at them. But now, from the open Border Police jeep, Gaza looked like a ghost town. There were four of them. Zanzuri drove, and apart from Stein, there was the sweaty black guy and a redhead. The redhead took a piece of Bazooka out of his vest pocket, put it in his mouth, and threw out the wrapper.

"Hey, Russki, toss a piece over here," Zanzuri demanded when he saw him in the rearview mirror.

"All gone," the redhead said and smiled, showing rotten teeth.

"Fuck," Zanzuri said and spat a wad of phlegm over the side of the jeep. "The first Arab I catch today is going to be one sorry son of a bitch!" The second jeep passed them. The driver was a skinny, scar-faced soldier, and the officer was in the passenger seat. A hundred meters in front of them, an old Arab man was trudging down the road. Stein saw Scar Face spin the wheel sharply to the left, lunge onto the sidewalk, and hit the old Arab, who landed on his face a few meters away and lay there motionless. "The mute's all hopped up today," Zanzuri said with a snicker. "Did you see how he sent the towel-head flying?" Stein, not understanding what exactly had happened, turned and saw the body on the sidewalk, saw Zanzuri laughing and the Russian chewing gum. He tried to put all the images together into a single, coherent reality, but he couldn't. The other jeep stopped at the corner of an alley, and Zanzuri pulled up right behind it.

Stein jumped out, ran over to the mute, and grabbed him by the shirt. "You ran him over on purpose, you psycho, you ran over a human being on purpose. He didn't do anything to you." The Russian grabbed Stein from behind with an iron grip and pulled him away from the mute.

"He didn't run over a human being," Zanzuri corrected. "He ran over an Arab, so what the fuck is your problem?" Stein felt the Russian's repulsive, hot breath on his neck and knew that if he opened his mouth to say something, he'd burst out crying.

"That roof there," the officer said, pointing, ignoring everything that had happened, "there's someone on it. I want Zanzuri and the Russki to bring him down here."

The Russian let go of Stein. He and Zanzuri disappeared into the alley the officer had pointed to. They were back two minutes later, dragging someone with his hands tied behind him and a wide strip of duct tape over his mouth.

"I shut him up," Zanzuri said. "I hate it when they start begging."

The mute sighed in agreement and nodded. He went over to the trussed-up Arab and pretended to bend down but straightened abruptly and butted him in the face.

"Did you find anything on him?" the officer asked in a bored tone.

"This!" Zanzuri said, proudly holding up a bottle of root beer with a soaked rag tied around its neck. "And he had a brick, too." The mute kept punching the Arab, who was now lying on the ground, moaning faintly.

"Enough!" Stein shouted, stepping toward them. The mute stood up, pulled his truncheon out of his vest, and glared at him.

"You're starting to get on my nerves, Stein," the officer muttered, an unlit cigarette in the corner of his mouth. He put the crushed pack of unfiltered Ascots into his pouch and rummaged around for something in his pocket. When he didn't find it, he went on: "What are you, Stein, the Red Cross? Those scum have only one thing on their minds—killing you. It's their only reason for living. Get that into your head. They might look like us on the outside, but they're not."

The Arab's bound body writhed on the ground, and Stein tried to go over and help him. The mute blocked his way.

"You just don't get it, do you?" the officer said. "Okay, like they say: a picture is worth a thousand words. Russki, pick him up," he ordered. The Russian stood the Arab up from the back and held on to him so he wouldn't fall. The Arab's face was caked with blood and dirt. "Zanzuri, the knife," the officer said, holding out his hand, the unlit cigarette still between his lips. Zanzuri took the knife out of his vest and slapped it into the officer's outstretched palm. The officer looked at the knife for a minute and tapped the handle with his finger. "The compass on the handle isn't working," he said.

"Yes, I know," Zanzuri said with a nod. "That asshole Bedouin broke it." He pointed at the black soldier, whose sweat-soaked uniform looked darker than the others.

"Fuck it," the officer said and ripped open the Arab's shirt. The buttons scattered on the ground, and Stein saw a hairy chest rising and falling rapidly.

"No!" Stein yelled, managing to take a step toward the officer. The mute smashed the back of his neck with the heavy wooden truncheon, and Stein fell to the ground.

"Hold him with his head up," Stein heard the officer command.

"Not the Arab, you moron," said the Russian, "the bleeding heart." He snickered.

Stein was on his knees now, the mute supporting him under an armpit with one hand, pulling his hair back with the other. Three meters away from him, the officer was moving the knife to the Arab's trembling stomach, and there was nothing he could do. With a quick slice, the officer cut the stomach in two, and rolled-up flags, flyers, candy, and phone tokens came spilling out of it.

"Don't touch the candy," the officer warned them. "It's poisoned." He handed the knife back to Zanzuri. The Russian unrolled one of the flags. It was a PLO flag. Zanzuri and the black soldier filled their pockets with phone tokens. The Russian stripped the Arab, who was lying on the ground flat as a sheet after being emptied out. He folded him in eight and laid him on the jeep's spare tire.

"Hey, Russki, what are you going to do with him?" Zanzuri asked.

"A cover for my motor scooter, a cape, who knows," said the Russian, and he shrugged. "It must be good for something."

"Man, those Russians are stingy," Zanzuri whispered to the black soldier, the tokens jingling in his pockets. Even though more than five minutes had gone by since the mute had hit him with his truncheon, Stein decided that the time had come to faint.

Stein woke up on his bed in the tent, wearing his clothes and shoes, the pain so agonizing that he could barely move his neck. Everyone was sleeping now. The needle of the broken compass on Zanzuri's knife handle glowed brightly in the dark. Stein got up quietly, pulled the knife out of its sheath, and started walking where the phosphorescent needle led him.

FREEZE!

Suddenly I could do it. I'd say "Freeze!" and everyone would freeze, just like that, in the middle of the street. Cars, bicycles, even those little motor scooters delivery guys use would stop in their tracks. And I'd walk past them looking for the hottest girls. I'd tell them to drop their shopping bags, I'd walk them off a bus, then I'd bring them home and fuck their brains out. It was great. Beyond great. "Freeze!" "Come here!" "Lie down on the bed!" And kablooey. These girls I had were knockouts, centerfolds. I was on top of the world. I felt like a king.

And then my mother started getting involved.

My mother told me she wasn't completely happy with the whole business. I told her there was no reason not to be happy. "I tell the girls to come and they come. It's not as if I rape them or anything."

And my mother said, "No, no. God forbid. It's just that there's something very impersonal about it. Unemotional. I don't know how to explain it, but I have this gut feeling that you don't really connect with them." So I told my mother that she could keep her gut feelings to herself. I told her that she could live her life and I'd live mine. I told her "Freeze!" and left her like that in the middle of Reiness Street in the pouring rain.

It pissed me off, her sticking her nose in my business.

Since then, it hasn't been the same. What she said bothered me, the part about not connecting. Now I fucked the girls like before, but I didn't really feel connected. Everything was ruined. At first I thought it was the sounds. So I'd say to the girls, "Make sounds." And they'd make all kinds of sounds: Mickey Mouse, jackhammers, politicians. It was a nightmare. I had to demonstrate the actual words I wanted them to say. "Oh yeah." "Do it to me, do it to me." "Harder." That kind of stuff. And they'd repeat them when we were fucking, but always in my intonation. "Don't stop. I'm coming," they'd say as they lay there motionless, eyes glazed. I knew they were lying, and it made me so mad I could've strangled them. "If you don't mean it, don't say it." I'd yell that a few times, but what was the use? It was depressing. Beyond depressing.

But then it came to me, what was fucking everything up. The problem was I was micromanaging. Once I figured that out, I started telling them more general things like "Act like you're really enjoying it," and when the feeling they were faking it started to bother me, I'd just say, "Enjoy it." It was terrific. Beyond terrific. They'd scream. They'd dig their nails into my back. They'd say, "You're the best." Can you picture it? Models, flight attendants, weather girls, in my bed, telling me I'm great.

Except that then, knowing they were there just because I said so started to bug me. It hit me out of the blue, like lightning. I was walking past Reiness Street, right where it hits Gordon.

My mother was still standing there with that apologetic look on her face exactly where I left her, and I suddenly understood: this wasn't the real thing, it never would be. Because none of those girls really appreciates me. None of them wants me for who I really am. And if they're not with me for who I am, then fuck it. Right then, I decided to stop and to hit on girls the regular way.

Boy did that suck. It was a flop, a fiasco, beyond terrible. Girls I used to fuck right in the street, right up against a mailbox, suddenly refused to give me their numbers. They started saying things like my breath stinks or I'm not their type or they have a boyfriend. It was grim. It was beyond grim. But I wanted a real relationship so bad that, even though the temptation to go back to fucking like I used to was enormous, I resisted.

After three months of torment, I saw the girl from the cider ads in the middle of Ibn Gvirol. I went up and tried to start a conversation, I told her a joke, I picked up a bouquet and ran after her with flowers in my hand, but she didn't even stop. Waiting for her in the lot beside the mall was this sporty little Mazda driven by another model, a guy model, the one from the potato chip ad. She was about to get into his car and drive away. I didn't know what to do, and without even realizing it, I yelled "Freeze!" She stopped in her tracks. Everyone did. I looked around at all the people frozen there like that, at her, as beautiful as she was in the commercials. I didn't know what to do. On the one hand, I couldn't, I just couldn't let her go. On the other, if she was going to be with me, I wanted it to be for who I am, because of my inner self, not because I ordered her to be. And then it came, the solution. Like an epiphany. I held her hand, looked into her eyes, and said, "Love me for who I am, for who I truly am." Then I took her back to my apartment and fucked her like a freak. She screamed and dug her nails into my back and said, "Do it, oh yes, do it to me." And she loved me, she loved me so much. Just for being me.

ALTERNATIVE

Suddenly, an alternative presented itself. An alternative that had always existed in theory but, for her at least, had always been out of reach. She remembered very well how, only six months ago, she had looked down from her balcony. And the thing that had stiffened her neck mumbled to her through her throat, "I don't understand how people do that to themselves." She just didn't understand. But now she does. Not that she has to do it, but the alternative exists. Like a driver's license, like a visa to the United States. Something she can take advantage of, or not.

There was a time when she wouldn't do that for guys—*suck them off, go down on them, give head, blow them*—it's interesting how all those names they invented for it sound so disgusting. Maybe it was the names that repulsed her. But not anymore. Not that she thought it was so great. But she could do it when she thought she should. Another alternative.

Then they're in bed and she has that aftertaste in her mouth. Kind of salty-sticky. Something between pretzels and fish.

He pulls her on top of him like he always does. Kisses her on the mouth. So he can taste it too. As if to prove that it isn't disgusting.

"What are you thinking about?" he asks.

She smiles, thinking about the alternative. "Nothing," she tells him, "nothing."

She wonders if there really is nothing afterward, or if there is something. Her intuition tells her there's nothing. Because if it's pretty much nothing now, when everything's moving, then it would probably be the same afterward. But not necessarily. There is no "necessarily." We have free choice. Nothing or not nothing. The alternatives are all in our hands.

They say she's gifted, but what do I know. I roam around her soul, and it's like a deserted apartment. Like a house where the parents have shoved all the furniture into a corner because their son is having a party. Gifted at painting, they say, and writing, too. Creative, but quiet and slightly odd. And I say—she's anybody's guess. Nothing here is clear. Because of her, I feel guilty.

I've always asked myself what girls think when they're doing it. Not suicide, the sex thing. It bothers me. I always used to think that they thought it was supposed to bum them out, to humiliate them. I hoped that, if I could get inside her head, everything would be different, I'd get some kind of insight. Different, my ass. This isn't why I became a writer.

She looks up from the balcony. The sky. Iron bars and the sky. Her thoughts—not sharp at all. The whole thing's kitsch. In the end, she'll die, even though they say she's gifted. She'll go down on me and she'll die. She'll die and she'll go down on me. In the name of free choice. In the name of the Movement for the Advancement of Women and Gravitation. And I can tie it all together neatly so the climax shows off my narrative skills. Or not.

WITHOUT HER

What do you do the day the woman of your life dies? I went to Jerusalem and back. There were terrible traffic jams; some film festival was opening. Just getting from downtown to the highway took more than an hour. The guy I was driving with was a young lawyer and an expert in one of those martial arts or something. "Thank you all," he mumbled to himself the whole way out of town. "Thank you to all the people who chose me, and especially to my mother. Without her . . . without her . . ." He always got stuck like that at "without her," all three hundred times.

Once we'd gotten out of town, and traffic started to flow, he stopped saying thank you and just kept staring at me. "Are you okay?" he asked every few seconds. "Are you okay?" And I said yes. "Are you sure?" he persisted. "Are you sure?" And I said yes again. I was a little hurt that he'd thanked everyone but me.

"So how about telling me something," he said. "Not any of that bullshit you make up, something that really happened to you." So I told him about the extermination.

My landlord threw in the extermination free of charge. He'd

handwritten it in at the bottom of the lease without my even asking for it. A week later, a guy with a plastic jerrican and a Dr. Roach shirt woke me up. He did the whole house in forty minutes and told me to air out the place when I came back that evening and not to wash the floors for a week. As if I would've washed them if he hadn't told me not to.

When I came home after work, there was no floor. Everything was covered with a carpet of legs turned to the ceiling. Three layers of corpses. One or two hundred per tile. Some were the size of kittens. One, its belly covered with white spots, was the size of a television. They weren't moving. I asked one of the neighbors for a spade and loaded them into jumbo-size garbage bags. When I'd filled something like fifteen of them, the room began to spin. My head hurt. I went to open all the windows, corpses crumbling under my feet. In the kitchen, I found one swinging from the light fixture. The bug must have realized it was going to die from the poison and decided to hang itself. I loosened the rope, and the body fell on me. I almost collapsed; it weighed about seventy kilos. It was wearing a black jacket, no pockets, and it didn't have any papers or a watch or anything, not even wings. It reminded me of someone I knew in the army. I felt really sorry for it.

I took the others downstairs in the bags, but I dug that one a grave. I found an empty watermelon crate near the Dumpster and put it on the grave instead of a headstone. A week later, the exterminator guy came to spray the place again, but I whacked him on the head with a kitchen chair and he was out of there in a flash. He didn't even stop to ask why.

When I'd finished telling the story, we were both quiet. Then

I asked him if it was true that a lawyer can't inform on his clients, and he said yes. I offered him a cigarette, but he didn't want one. I turned on the news, but the announcers were on strike.

"Tell me," he finally asked, "if it wasn't for the festival, how come you wanted to go to Jerusalem?"

"No reason," I said. "A woman I knew died."

"Knew her for no reason, or died for no reason?" he persisted. Then came the Shalom intersection, and instead of taking a right, he spun the wheel left, straight into the median.

SIDEWALKS

arrived a week later, the way I always do. I never come on the actual date. I did go to the funeral and to the first memorial, but with all those people staring, the firm handclasps, the mother smiling at me teary-eyed and asking me when I was finishing my degree—I said fuck it. The date itself doesn't mean much to me anyway, though it's an easy one to remember: December 12, the twelfth day of the twelfth month.

Ronen's sister is a doctor at Beilinson Hospital, and she was on duty the moment your heart stopped. I heard Ronen tell Yizhar that you died at the stroke of noon. Like, on the dot.

Ronen got all worked up about it: "On the twelfth of the twelfth at twelve. Do you realize what the odds are?" he whispered so loud that everyone could hear. "It's like an omen from Heaven."

"Incredible," Yizhar muttered. "If he'd stuck around another twelve minutes and twelve seconds, I bet they'd have issued a stamp in his honor or something."

It really is easy to remember—the date, I mean—and the street sign we stole together on Yom Kippur. And that retarded boomerang they brought you from Australia, the one we used to throw in the park when we were kids and it never came back. Every year I come and stand beside the grave and think back, remembering something else each time, remembering very clearly. We'd each had five beers, and then you did another three shots of vodka. I was feeling pretty okay that night. Tipsy, but okay. You? You were shitfaced. We left the pub for your place, a few hundred meters away. We were wearing those gray raincoats we'd bought together at the pedestrian mall. You were pretty wobbly, and you knocked into a phone pole with your shoulder. You took a step back and stared—bemused is how you looked. I shut my eyes, and the blackness of my lowered eyelashes swirled together with the dark vapors of the alcohol. I tried to picture you far away from me, in a different country, say, and the thought scared me so much that my eyes snapped open, just in time for me to see you take another unsteady step and tip over backward. I caught you just before you hit the ground, and you smiled at me with your head tilted back, like a kid who's discovered a new game.

"We won," you told me, as I helped you up. I had no idea what you were talking about. Then we took a few more steps and you did it again, deliberately this time. You just let your body drop forward, and I grabbed you by the coat collar, a tenth of a second before your face hit the sidewalk.

"Two–zip," you said and leaned against me. "We're good. The sidewalks haven't got a chance."

———

We kept walking toward your house, and every few steps you let yourself drop to the sidewalk, and every time I'd catch you—by the belt, by the waist, by the hair. Never letting you touch the ground. "Six–zip," you said, and then "Nine–zip." The game kicked ass, and so did we. We were unbeatable.

"Let's hold them at zero," I whispered in your ear, and that's just what we did. By the time we reached your house, we'd scored an amazing twenty-one to nothing. We entered the building, leaving the humiliated sidewalks behind us. Your roommate was there in your apartment, sitting up and watching TV.

"We fucked them up," you said as we walked in, and he rubbed his eyes behind his glasses and said we looked like shit. I was about to wash my face, but before I even made it to the sink I threw up in the bathtub. I heard you screaming in the hallway that you weren't about to piss in that configuration. I came out of the bathroom and saw you staggering, with your pants down to your knees.

"I'm not going to piss with you holding me up," you told your roommate. "You I don't trust. Only him. I want him to hold me," you said, pointing at me. "Only him."

"It's nothing personal," I said and smiled at the roommate. "It's just that we have lots of practice." I helped you up by the waist.

"You're fucking insane." The roommate shook his head and went back to his show. You finished pissing. I threw up another time. On the way to your bed, you fell once more, and I caught you, just barely, and both of us fell to the floor. "I knew you'd catch me," you said and laughed.

"Look," you said and tried to get up again. "I've lost my fear of falling. My fear of falling's gone."

There are these two kids here at your grave, aiming their tennis ball at the tombstones. I think I've figured out the rules: if the one they hit is an officer's, they get a point. If it's a cadet's, it's a point for the cemetery. They hit your tombstone, and the ball rebounded right into my hand. I caught it. One of the kids walked toward me apprehensively.

"Are you the guard?" I shook my head. "So, can we get our ball back?" He took another step in my direction.

I handed him the ball. He moved up closer to the tombstone, squinting at it.

"SFC," he called out to his friend, who was standing a ways away.

"What's SFC?" the faraway one asked. The one with the ball shrugged.

"Excuse me," he asked. "Is SFC an officer or just a normal soldier?" "An officer, of course," I said. "It stands for Super First Commander."

"Yes!" he shouted and hurled the ball high in the air. "Eight–seven!" His friend came running and yelled, "We beat the gravestones! We beat the gravestones!" and the two of them started jumping and yelling like they'd just taken the world championship, or better.

SLIMY SHLOMO IS A HOMO

The sub told them to line up in pairs. Slimy Shlomo Is a Homo was the odd man out. "I'll be your partner," the sub said and gave him her hand.

Then they went for a walk in the park, and Slimy Shlomo Is a Homo looked at the boats in the artificial lake, and at a gigantic sculpture of an orange, and then a bird pooped on his hat.

"Shit sticks to shit," Yuval shouted at them from behind, and the other kids laughed.

"Ignore them," the sub said and rinsed his hat off under a faucet. Next came the ice-cream man, and everyone bought ice cream. Slimy Shlomo Is a Homo ate his Popsicle, and when he finished, he pushed the stick between the tiles in the pavement and pretended it was a rocket. The other kids were fooling around on the grass, and only Slimy Shlomo Is a Homo and the sub, who was smoking a cigarette and looking pretty tired, stayed on the pavement.

"Why do all the kids hate me?" Slimy Shlomo Is a Homo asked her.

"How should I know?" The sub shrugged her drooping shoulders. "I'm just a sub."

TERMINAL

Hans and I had nothing in common except brain cancer. He was a shriveled-up old guy who spoke broken Hebrew, and I'm a fat, overgrown sabra still on this side of forty. Even so, and although we were roommates less than a month, we felt like old friends. "Is because you and me, we both terminal sick," Hans explained. I loved his fractured Hebrew, especially when he called me "terminal sick," like I'm waiting at some busy airport about to take off for an exciting, different place.

We used to play chess. Hans was once on the Mainz University team and even won the university championship in 1935. "But now, because cancer in my head, I how you say, *idiotish*?" Me? I was an idiot even before the cancer. Sometimes Hans would forget to move when it was his turn, and he'd just sit there staring into space until I nudged him. "Pardon," he'd apologize and make his move quickly. I also had blackouts when we were playing, sometimes I'd even forget how to move the pieces, mainly the knight, and Hans would remind me with his usual patience.

Dr. Arad says that forgetting is perfectly natural in advanced stages of brain cancer, which must've been meant to reassure me.

Everyone always says that the *yekkim*, the German Jews, are as dry as dust, but with Hans at least, that wasn't true. The guy was a straight-out poet. Like the time he told me about Bergen-Belsen, "I remember the day they take Anna and little Karl. I just not know what will happen next minute. I look at my watch and I know: five minutes more the tram come, forty minutes more I hug Anna, make little Karl to laugh, everything be in order. All of sudden, I am on bed, alone, not know anything what will happen. I want killing myself, only so I be sure of something."

Hans froze and stared at the wall across from him, and for a minute I thought it was another attack, he forgot what he was talking about. "Then I see him on wall," he went on, "*mein Schatten*, how you say, aah . . . shadow. I look at him and I know, my shadow he always with me. I know always what he is going to do, and him even the Germans they cannot take." Hans raised his hand and stared at its giant shadow on the wall making the exact same gesture. He looked at me and smiled. "*Zauber*," he whispered.

Hans was in worse shape than me, and when his urine bag had to be emptied, I did it. "Pardon," he'd always say, apologizing as if it was his fault he was sick. The truth is that Asher, the orderly, was supposed to empty urine bags, but that bastard liked to drop in only once a day, to change the soaked sheets. I always cursed under my breath when that shit finally showed up in the ward, and it was Hans who defended him. "Not to be angry, Zvi, he is *jünger Mensch*, he has much life yet and we are at end."

———

Once, Hans asked me what the name Zvi meant. I didn't know how to explain it. Finally, I showed him a picture of the deer in the Israeli Postal Authority logo printed on the envelope of a letter I'd gotten. "Ah, *Hirsch*, beautiful animal, but not many now, almost extinct." I told him that people with brain cancer who play chess are probably almost extinct too, and he looked at the drawing of the deer again, a gentle smile flitting across his face.

Funny, the whole time we were together I was aware that death could come and take me at any time. But I never thought that the same death could visit Hans, too. It never entered what was left of my mind that a man who talks so funny could die. When it happened, I was really calm. I didn't cry, didn't yell, nothing. Asher came in. "What's the name of the old guy who died?" he asked. "Dr. Arad needs it for the death certificate and the nurses lost the papers again. Wasn't it Hindisheim, Hindishtreim, something like that?" Remembering what Hans said about his shadow, I looked at the wall and raised my right hand high, like Hans. That sneaky little shadow rebelled and decided to put his hands around the shadow of someone else's neck. I couldn't even trust my shadow now. Asher grunted and screamed. I heard other people's voices. I kept looking at the mutinous shadow. I want killing myself. Then my lips chose to utter a word I didn't know the meaning of. *"Zauber,"* I heard myself whisper.

JOURNEY

You're sure this isn't the way?" Daniel asked haltingly. "I see some lights in the distance." The scout kept walking in silence, and Daniel, as if having no choice, trudged behind him. This stillness droning on around them was unnerving, oppressive. He would have given a lot for the scout to say something. But the scout marched on wordlessly, and Daniel found himself impelled to speak. "My parents wanted me to study law or accounting, you know. My grades were pretty good. I got into this prelaw program, no problem," Daniel said, trying to make eye contact with the scout, whose gaze, however, remained fixed on the ground. Warily he examined every track as if it led to a snare.

"But I asked myself, Why should I be buried under a pile of books, in the fluorescent basement of some library," Daniel went on, although by then he knew he wasn't about to get an answer. "I'm still young. The world's my oyster, and it's full of things nobody's ever seen. Places just waiting for me to show up. Like here, for instance." Daniel held out his arms, as if trying to embrace the strange landscape around him.

"Not quite here yet. Pretty soon." They were the first words the scout had spoken.

"Sorry," Daniel said, more softly. "I got carried away."

On they walked. To Daniel, the silence was heavier than the rucksack on his back. He paused to wipe the sweat from his forehead and found himself speaking again, this time in a whisper. "Two months after I got out of the army I went to Thailand, to look for all those hidden places, you know." He stopped and sighed. The scout didn't even turn around. "Everywhere I went I found trekkers, like me, each convinced he was on his way to discovering a new continent." He shook his head as if in disbelief. "Every hostel, every waterfall, every palm tree was teeming with tourists: Swedes, Germans, Israelis. Especially Israelis. All looking for virgin territory, and making do in the end with a game of cards and a few rounds of gin and orange juice. The Far East, it's one big campground."

The scout paused, raised his hand to his neck, and froze. At first, Daniel thought the scout was mulling over what he'd just said. But once the scout had studied the stars, he resumed walking, leading Daniel across the smooth, open sands. "Then I went to South America," Daniel continued. "There I thought I stood a chance of finding the place. Some new place to call my own. But there, too, everywhere I went there were people smoking Camels, always slapping you on the back, asking you where in Israel you're from, what unit you served in. I couldn't take it anymore. I grabbed my rucksack and headed into the jungle, just like that. No compass, no map, no guide. I let myself get lost. For days I just wandered. I didn't give a single thought to food, mosquitoes, snakes, anything. I was alone. And then I reached a clearing in the forest. In the center there was this enormous tree, standing all on its own. I decided that this clearing would be my home. That would be where I'd live. Just me and the tree. 'I'm Robinson Crusoe,' I told the tree. 'Who are you?' It didn't answer." Daniel chuckled. "Just like you. Maybe it preferred life on its own, without me. I circled it a few times, touched its trunk, its branches. Next to the base of the trunk I discovered an almost invisible scar. I bent down to check it out. Imagine my shock. Someone had carved something with a penknife. The bark had grown back and tried to conceal it, but I could make out all of the words: NIR DEKEL, AUGUST 5, PARATROOPERS KICK ASS. I hoisted up my rucksack and started walking, looking around me at the jungle. The tree limbs seemed to be slapping me on the back, the crocodiles winked and wanted to know where I'd done my ser-vice, the scorpions were about to pour me a screwdriver. The entire jungle suddenly looked like one big practical joke Nir Dekel had set up for me. I knew I'd wind up in the city eventually. The world had become so small you couldn't get lost. Not if you were an amateur. I actually burst into tears."

Daniel took a long breath, letting the sea air into his lungs. "And that's pretty much it. I came back home, retook the boards, and registered for class." He glanced at his watch. "I had four days to go when they told me about you, how you get people lost, how you're a pro—"

"We're here," the scout announced and came to a halt.

Daniel looked around him, confused. "Here? But you can see the lights from here. You can hear the people. Look, there's the power station," he said, pointing at the lit-up chimney.

"It may seem close, but nobody has ever come here," the

scout declared firmly, crouching to take a close look at the tar-soaked earth. "And nobody ever will."

"So close to Tel Aviv and yet nobody will ever come here? How is that possible?"

"Fucked if I know." The scout shrugged and gave Daniel a wink. "Maybe they're all in Thailand."

"And what about me? I'm bound to find the way back to Tel Aviv from here."

"You could try." The scout smiled, then he straightened up, turned his back to Daniel, and moved off. His light steps left no tracks in the sand. The next thing Daniel knew, he was gone.

NOTHING

And she loved a man who was made of nothing. A few hours without him and right away she'd be missing him with her whole body, sitting in her office surrounded by polyethylene and concrete and thinking of him. And every time she'd boil water for coffee in her ground-floor office, she'd let the steam cover her face, imagining it was him stroking her cheeks, her eyelids, and she'd wait for the day to be over, so she could go to her apartment building, climb the flight of stairs, turn the key in the door, and find him waiting for her, naked and still between the sheets of her empty bed.

Nothing in the world would have made her happier than to make love with him all night long, tasting his non-lips once again, feeling the uncontrollable quiver run through him, the emptiness spread through her body. He wasn't her first. There'd been many before him, sweating and moaning in her bed, squeezing her till it hurt, their fleshy tongues in her mouth, in her throat, almost choking her. Different men, made of different ingredients: of flesh and blood, of fears, of their fathers' credit cards, of treachery, of longing for someone else . . . But that was then. Now she had him. Sometimes, after they made love, they'd go for a walk in the night-soaked streets. Holding each other, sharing a single poncho, oblivious to the winds and the rain, as if inured to their touch. He took no notice of what people were saying around them, and she pretended not to hear either. None of the gossip or the nastiness could touch their world.

She knew her parents weren't happy about her beloved, even though they hid it. She once even overheard her father whisper to her mother, "Better than an Arab—or a junkie." Of course they'd have been happier if she were going out with a gifted doctor instead, or a young lawyer. Parents like to take pride in their daughter, and that's hard to do with a man who's made of nothing. Even when the man made her happy, filling her life with meaning, more than any man made of something could.

They could spend hours together, wrapped in each other's arms, never saying a word, lying there naked with no change in their love or their position. And when the clock began urging her out of bed, she'd skip her morning coffee, skip washing her face or brushing her hair, for just a few more minutes of being together, with him. And all the way down the stairs, to the bus stop, to where she worked, she'd wait for the minute she'd turn the key in the door, and there he'd be. She hadn't the slightest doubt or apprehension. She knew that this love would never betray her. What could possibly let her down when she opened the door? An empty apartment? A numbing silence? An absence between the sheets of the rumpled bed?

MYTH MILK

They shot him like a dog, and me they slapped. That's how it always is—they shoot the men like dogs, and the women get slapped. "I don't have the heart to kill you even though you deserve it," said their leader, who, oddly enough, was the shortest one. "We won't even rape you," he added, and from the look in his eyes, I could tell that he considered himself a prince, but instead of thanking him for his courtesy, I started to cry. It's tough being a woman, what with all those slaps and all the men you lose. When you're a man, they take you out of bed in the middle of the night once, drag you into the street, and bam, it's over. But when you're a woman, it never ends. "It's natural to cry," he said, stroking my head, "it's the shock." And then he said again, "We won't even rape you. Even though you deserve it." Then they went away. It wasn't because they were afraid, men aren't afraid of anything. Maybe I wasn't grateful enough. I took the shovel out of the tool chest and dug a hole where the ground was soft. It took me three hours, and I got calluses on my hands. It's hard to dig a hole big enough for a person, especially a huge one like my man. I lugged his body to the hole, but I didn't have the strength left to cover him with sand, so I covered him with our flowered quilt and put the espresso machine we got from the kids for our last anniversary on top so the quilt wouldn't blow away. It's an old trick; my mother did the same when my father died. Then I went into the kitchen and took a carton of myth milk out of the refrigerator, drank two glasses, and gave a little hiccup, a woman's hiccup. When he hiccuped, the whole house used to shake. "Don't be a pig," I'd tell him, and he'd laugh. I went to bed, but it was hard to fall asleep without a man, even harder without the quilt on such a cold night. When I finally did, I dreamed they dragged us out of the house in the middle of the night and shot me like a dog, and for once, he was the one who got stuck with the slap and the "we won't rape you" and the grave and the myth milk, and it got me so excited that I woke up all wet, the way only a woman can.

THE NIGHT THE
BUSES DIED

I was waiting on the bench at the bus stop the night they died. Checking the punch marks in my bus pass, trying to figure out what they reminded me of. One of the holes looked like a rabbit. That one was my favorite. The others, no matter how long I stared at them, just kept looking like holes.

"An hour we've been waiting," an old man grumbled, half asleep. "Longer. The bus company, those two-faced fucks, when it comes to sponging off the government, they show up in no time, but when you're waiting for them to come—you could die first." Having said his piece, the old man adjusted his beret and went back to sleep. I smiled at his shut eyes and went back to staring at the holes, waiting patiently for something to change.

A sweaty young man flew past. Hardly breaking stride, he turned to us and gave a hoarse, breathless shout: "No point waiting. The buses are dead. All dead." He dashed off and had run quite a ways before he clutched his side with his left hand and turned to look back at us, as if remembering something important he'd forgotten to say. The tears on his cheeks glistened like beads of sweat. "All of them—all dead," he wailed, then turned back and he was gone.

The old man awoke with a start. "What does he want, the *meshugener*?"

"Nothing," I mumbled. I picked my backpack up off the ground and headed down the street.

"Hey there, young man, where are you going?" I heard the old man shouting behind me.

By the old chocolate factory there was a couple waiting, playing one of those finger games whose rules I've never figured out. "Hey," the guy called out to me. The pad of the girl's thumb was touching his outstretched palm. "Any idea what's up with the buses?"

I shrugged.

"Maybe there's a strike," I heard him tell her. "You'd better stay over, it's already pretty late."

The strap of my backpack was cutting into my back, and I straightened it out. All the way down the main drag the bus stops stood deserted. Everyone seemed to have given up and gone home. There hadn't been any outcry over the fact that the buses never came. I continued south.

On Ben-Gurion Avenue I saw my first corpse. It was lying on its back, badly bent out of shape. A thick smear of black brake oil covered the fragmented windshield. I knelt down and wiped at the oil with my shirtsleeve. It was a number 42. I'd never actually taken that one. I think it runs from Petah Tikva, or somewhere around there. A bus, gutted and prone in the middle of

Ben-Gurion Avenue. I didn't quite know how to account for the sadness I felt.

At the central bus station there were hundreds scattered all over the place, rivulets of fuel oozing out of their disemboweled shells, their shattered innards strewn on the black and silent asphalt. Dozens of people were sitting around, downcast, just waiting to hear the purr of a motor, their tearful eyes scouring the landscape in search of a spinning wheel. Someone in a bus inspector's hat was walking through the crowd, trying to offer some hope: "It's probably just here. There've got a whole fleet in Haifa. They'll be here any minute. Everything's going to be fine." But everybody—including him—knew that none had been spared.

People were saying that the *malabi* vendor had set fire to his cart, that the cassettes at the music stands had cracked in agony, that soldiers who'd been waiting at the station with bloodshot eyes weren't smiling as they walked back home. Even they were sad. I found an abandoned bus stop bench, lay down, and closed my eyes. The punch marks in my ticket still looked like ordinary holes.

MORAL SOMETHING

The guy on TV said the military court gave the death sentence to the Arab who'd killed the girl soldier, and lots of
people came on TV to talk about it, and because of that
the news went on till ten-thirty and they didn't show *Moonlight-
ing*. It made Dad so angry he lit his pipe in the house and it
stank. He's not supposed to do that because it stunts my growth.
He yelled at Mom that because of her and the other lunatics who
voted Likud the country was becoming just like Iran. And Dad
said we were going to pay for it, and that it was eroding our
moral something—I don't remember the word—whatever that
means, and that the U.S. wouldn't put up with it either.

The next day, they talked to us about it at school, and
Tziyyon Shemesh said that if you hang a guy he pops a boner,
like in porn, so Tzilla, our homeroom teacher, kicked him out.
Then she said different people feel different ways about the
death penalty, and no matter what arguments you make for it or
against it, people would have to decide in their heart. And Tzachi
the retard, who was left back two times, started laughing and
said the Arabs would have to decide in their heart after it

stopped beating, so Tzilla kicked him out too. And she said she wouldn't listen to any more nonsense and she was just going to teach us our regular subjects, and she got back at us with a ton of homework.

After school, the big kids had a fight about how if you hang somebody and he dies, it's because he chokes or the rope breaks his neck. Then they started betting cartons of chocolate milk and caught a cat and they hanged it from the basketball hoop, and the cat was screaming, and in the end its neck really did break. But Mickie's a cheap-ass, and he wouldn't pay for the chocolate milk, and he said it was because Gabi had jerked on the cat and that he wanted a do-over with a new cat that nobody touched. But everyone knew it was because he was a cheap-ass, so he had to pay. Then Nissim and Ziv said they should beat up Tziyyon Shemesh because he was a liar because the cat didn't get a boner. And Michal—she's the prettiest girl in the school, probably—came by and she said we were all disgusting and like animals, and I barfed but not because of her.

HAPPY BIRTHDAY
TO YOU

The bus stops, the driver smiles at you, the windows are gleaming, and you've got plenty of small change. In the row of single seats on the left, the last one is vacant as if it has your name on it, your favorite one. The bus pulls out, the lights turn green as it approaches, and the guy cracking sunflower seeds gathers up the shells in a brown paper bag.

The elderly inspector doesn't ask to see your ticket, just tips his hat and, in a very pleasant voice, wishes you a nice day.

And it will be a nice day. Because it's your birthday. You're bright, you're pretty, and you have your whole life ahead of you. Four more stops and you'll pull the cord, and the driver will stop, just for you.

You'll get off the bus, no one will jostle you, and the door won't close till you've stepped down. And the bus will leave, the passengers will be happy for you, and the guy with the sunflower seeds will keep waving goodbye, for no reason at all, till he's out of sight.

Who needs a reason, it's a birthday, and on birthdays nice things happen. And the puppy running toward you now will wag its tail when you pet it. When it's a really special date, even dogs can tell.

In your apartment, people will be waiting in the dark, behind the beautiful furniture the two of you chose yourselves. When you open the door, they'll jump out and shout "Surprise!" And you'll be perfectly surprised.

They'll all be there, the people you've loved. Those closest to you, and the ones who mean the most. And they'll bring presents that they bought or dreamed up themselves. Inspired presents, and useful things too.

The funny ones will entertain, the smart ones will edify, even the melancholy ones will smile and mean it. The food will be amazing, then they'll serve strawberries and top it off with vanilla milk shakes from the best ice-cream parlor in town.

They'll play a Keith Jarrett disc and everyone will listen, they'll play a record and nobody will feel sad. And the ones who are on their own won't feel alone tonight, and nobody will ask "Milk or cream?" because by now they'll all know one another.

In the end they'll leave, and the ones you wanted to kiss you will kiss you, and the ones you didn't will just shake your hand. And he'll be the only one who'll stay behind, the man you live with, kinder and gentler than ever.

If you want to, you'll make love or he'll massage your body in oil, something he picked out just for you in an old Bedouin shop. He'll dim the halogen light—all you have to do is ask—and you'll sit there enfolded in his arms, waiting for dawn.

And on that magical night, I'll be there too, drinking my vanilla milk shake and smiling a genuine smile. And before I go, if you want, I'll kiss you. And if not, I'll just shake your hand.

THE BACKGAMMON
MONSTER

For Uzi, the greatest Ashkenazi backgammon player of all time

D ouble," the backgammon monster bellowed like a wounded animal, its voice thick with menace and imprecation. "Double," it cried again. Passersby stopped in their tracks, and the heads of curious neighbors appeared at their windows. The entire street froze. The only sound to be heard was the rattle of dice. "Double," the backgammon monster cried a third time, now in a whisper, then touched its clenched fist to the yarmulke on its head and cast the dice against the side of the board in total concentration, as if aiming at some invisible target. Even before the dice had settled on the board, Lior knew he'd lost. "Four-four," the monster said. "You owe me a candy bar." It got up and went to stack the tomatoes.

"I'm not at all happy that our Liori is spending his whole allowance gambling," Lior's mother complained. "Would it hurt him to go to an after-school activity? Sarah's Yaniv plays the accordion, the Stein boy is learning computers. And my son has to spend his afternoons playing primitive games with a criminal who sells fruit and vegetables—"

"Ziva, you're exaggerating," said Lior's father, interrupting her diatribe. "David's a religious man, not a criminal, and I can't see anything wrong with every now and then playing a game—"

"No? *Not a criminal?* To take a naïve little boy's last penny? And that scar that covers half his face—what, you think he got that shaving?"

"Really, Ziva, it's a fair and friendly game. For God's sake, don't blow it out of proportion. They only play for candy bars, after all."

"If it's so fair, then how come Lior never wins . . ."

And once again she was off.

To anyone else, it would have seemed an unremarkable day. Bright sun, light breeze, nothing out of the ordinary. But Lior knew the day was special. The dice in his hand kept whispering six-six, and the pieces aligned themselves on the board exactly the way he wanted. A woman came into the store and asked for cucumbers. "No cucumbers," the backgammon monster told her. "We're closed."

"What do you mean? You have piles of cucumbers here, and it's only five o'clock—"

"Lady," the backgammon monster shouted, the vein in the middle of its sweaty forehead threatening to burst, "we're playing now. The store is closed."

"My son's coming home from camp today," the woman ventured, "and he loves his cucumber soup, especially in this heat—"

"Closed!" the monster repeated, staring hard at the board. As it did so, it unconsciously fell to stroking the handle of the watermelon knife at its left.

"You're right, Mr. Zviti," the woman conceded. "It won't kill him for once to eat a schnitzel. These kids today are spoiled."

She left. The dice rolled on, doing whatever Lior wanted, and a new smell wafted in the air above the fragrances of onions and kohlrabi. It was the smell of victory.

"Double," Lior piped in his shrill voice, waving his fists in the monster's scowling face. "Double," he repeated, giving the obedient dice their command. For a second they spun irresolutely, as if contemplating rebellion, but thought better of it and came to rest. "Five-five. Triple win," Lior said. "You owe me three candy bars." Then he got up and went to eat a plum.

"Watch the store a minute," the monster said and went out the door, its shoulders stooped. When it returned it was just plain David, holding three candy bars in his hand. "Today you got lucky. Don't get used to it," David said. But no vein-in-the-forehead or touching-the-yarmulke tricks would ever help again. The backgammon monster had been vanquished.

ON THE NUTRITIONAL VALUE OF DREAMS

I woke up in the middle of the night, startled to find the Geshternak eating a dream I was having about you. Furious, I jumped out of bed and punched it in the nose as hard as I could. The Geshternak dropped what was left of the dream, but I didn't stop hitting it. Even when it crawled under the bed and lost its shape, I kept punching that ungainly shadow. Finally I stopped. Exhausted and sweaty, I gathered up the remnants of the dream. It didn't leave much, just the black sweatpants you were wearing, your effortless grin, and a certain contact between us, I don't know what kind—maybe a hug. The Geshternak had eaten everything around it, leaving only that, naked. I was left sprawled on the floor, desolate and silent, in nothing but my boxers and a layer of sweat. Hours of patient sleep, waiting for the dream to come. And now—nothing, worse than nothing, just a single drop of the taste of a vanished ice pop dripping into my mouth. A faint whimper came from under the bed. It was the Geshternak. First I thought it might be in pain—after all, I'd really walloped the shadow—but there wasn't an ounce of pain in the sobs. I tasted the Geshternak's tears, which were flowing along the bedroom floor, and they were sweet on my tongue; the Geshternak was crying with joy, and its tears attested to the wonderful taste of the dream, which was making every bit of its nonexistent body tremble. Its sobs told me about those long nights it had waited under the bed, empty, feeding only on fragments of my dreams. Nauseating dreams of boredom and apathy it had no choice but to chew on slowly; dreams of pain, loss, and fear it tried to destroy so I could sleep; dreams that so often stuck painfully in its throat. Every night, the Geshternak swallowed hour after hour of indifference and suffering, leaving my sleep smooth and dark, and tonight, it finally got its reward. Its painful hunger was satisfied, and for a while, it had experienced the alternative to emptiness. Its body knew more than nothingness. It was almost sunrise, and my partner's shadow hand slid out from under the bed and pointed to the middle of the room, to the bits of the dream I still had left—sweatpants, a smile, an intoxicating, elusive touch—and the fading fingers of the shadow seemed to be saying, "Here, my friend, there's some good left for you, too."

MONKEY SAY,
MONKEY DO

Have a banana," she begged. I don't want to.

"Come on, sweetheart. Show the nice man how you eat a banana." Let the nice man eat the banana. I'm through with this, for good.

"Excuse me, Dr. Gonen, but this is completely unacceptable. Dragging me all the way out from Sydney just to watch him sitting there in his cage with his eyes shut, shrugging his shoulders. My time is very precious, you know, and I won't have it wasted on one pretext and ano—"

"I'm sorry, Professor Strum, I have no idea what's gotten into him. It looks as if he may be upset by all this commotion. He's not used to strangers. If you'd just please wait outside for a few minutes, I know I can get him to respond."

Don't be so sure, honeybunch. Don't be so sure.

"Five minutes," he says, and I hear him walking away. "Five minutes." The door shuts, and a key turns in the lock.

"Please, lover," she says, stroking my fur. "Talk to the man, show him how smart you are." Her hand is touching my balls now, and my penis begins to stiffen. But I don't open my eyes.

"Really, sweetheart," she says and goes on stroking. "Do this for me. Otherwise they'll close down the project . . ."

Silence.

". . . and then we won't be able to stay together anymore."

So we won't. I've got my pride, haven't I? The strokes come faster now. It feels so good. But I don't open my eyes, don't say a word, don't give in.

"The five minutes are up, Dr. Gonen," comes the voice from behind the locked door. I open my eyes just a crack. She notices, stops stroking and brings her face up close.

"If that's the way you want it, that's the way you'll have it," she whispers. She removes her barrette and lets her hair down. It falls to her shoulders. She runs her fingers through it. She's an attractive woman.

"There are lots of professors around here who'd love a chance to saw your head open and look inside your brain," she says. "I'm through with you. From now on, you're all theirs."

"Dr. Gonen," comes the voice from outside again, and there's a tug at the handle of the locked door.

"Professor Strum," she whispers through the door and turns the key. "Please, call me Yael."

Before she opens the door, she undoes the top button of her blouse.

"Yael," the voice repeats from the other side of the door.

Her lips move, quietly, but I can hear her. "Stupid monkey," she says.

GULLIVER IN ICELANDIC

On my first day, I was overcome with dread. It wasn't even four in the afternoon and the sun had set long ago. They turn on the streetlamps here by two, two-thirty, and in the brief spell of sunshine, the colors are as dim as in an old photo.

For five months now I've been traveling on my own, just me and my knapsack, looking at snow and fjords and ice. The whole world is painted white, and at night—it's black. Sometimes I have to remind myself this is just a trek. "Look, a lemming!" I tell myself, and I force myself to pull out a camera. But how many pictures can one guy take? In my heart, I feel like an exile.

I blow hot air into my thick gloves, steam that's supposed to drive away the cold. But the cold that escapes lingers in the air, and as soon as the steam is gone, it's back. The cold here isn't like the cold back home. It's a cold that goes beyond temperatures. A sneaky cold that works its way through every layer and freezes you from inside.

I keep walking down the street. There's a small bookstore on the left, and the lights are on inside. It's been six months since I've read a book. I go in. It's nice and warm in there. "Excuse me," I say. "Do you have any books in English?" The cashier shakes his head and goes back to reading his ugly-lettered newspaper. I'm in no hurry to leave. I stroll down the aisles. I study the covers and breathe in the smell of the crisp paper. There's a nun standing next to one of the shelves. From behind, she looks for a moment like Death in the Bergman film. But I muster my courage and walk over to the shelf nearby to steal a glance at her. She has a thin and pretty face. Very pretty. I know the book she's holding. I recognize it by the picture on the cover. She puts it back in its place and moves on to a different one. I pull it out quickly. It's still warm as I hold it. It's *Gulliver*—*Gulliver* in Icelandic, but still *Gulliver*. It has the same cover as the Hebrew edition. We had it at home. I think someone gave it to my brother as a present. I pay the cashier. He insists on gift-wrapping it for me. He sticks a pink ribbon on the colorful wrapping and curls it with one of the blades of his scissors. Why not, actually? It's a gift for myself.

As soon as I leave the store, I tear off the wrapping, remove my knapsack and lean it against a streetlamp, then sit down on the snow-covered sidewalk and start to read. I know the book well, and even if I've forgotten something, the pictures are there to remind me. The book is the same one, and the words are the same too. Even if I'm the one who makes them up. And *Gulliver* in Icelandic is still *Gulliver*, a book I like a lot. I'm so worked up, I start to sweat. It's the first time I've sweated since I got here. My bulky coat and damp gloves make it difficult for me to turn the pages, so I get rid of them. The first two books are terrific, and I enjoy the third one too. But one thing's for sure: his last journey is the most impressive of all. I've always wanted to be like those noble Houyhnhnms. When Gulliver is forced to abandon them and return to the humans, I start crying and I can't stop. I finish the book and notice that the streetlamp isn't on anymore. In the headlights of a passing car, I see a figure in black beside me. The lights freeze, but the cold stopped bothering me long ago. The figure turns toward me. It's him, there's no mistaking that scythe, that skeleton face. For a moment, from behind, it looked just like a nun.

CHEERFUL COLORS

Danny was about six years old the first time he came across the Weekly Paint-by-Color. The children were supposed to help Uncle Isaac find his lost pipe and to color it in with cheerful colors. Danny found the pipe, colored it in with cheerful colors, and even won the prize that was raffled off among those who had solved it correctly—a *National Landscapes* encyclopedia. That was just the beginning. Danny helped Yoav find his puppy, Hero, and helped Yael and Bilha find their baby sister, and helped Policeman Avner find his missing pistol, and Amir and Ami the soldiers find their missing patrol jeep, and he always made sure to color things in with cheerful colors.

He helped Yair the hunter find the hidden rabbit and helped the Roman soldiers find Jesus, and helped Charles Manson find Sharon Tate, who was hiding in the bedroom, and helped Sergeant Jones find Saddam Hussein, who was at large, and he did it all without ever forgetting to color them in with cheerful colors.

He knew people called him Snitch behind his back, but he didn't care. He went right on helping. He helped George find

Noriega, who'd been lying low, and helped the Nazi henchmen find Anne Frank, and helped the Romanian people find the elusive Ceauşescu, and always made sure to color the fugitives with cheerful colors.

Terrorists and freedom fighters the world over realized it was no use hiding. Some of them, in sheer desperation, even colored themselves in cheerful colors. All in all, most people lost faith in their power to fight against their destiny. The world became a pretty depressing place. Danny himself wasn't very happy either. Searching and coloring didn't interest him anymore, and only inertia kept him going. Besides, he no longer had anywhere to store the seven hundred twenty-eight copies of the *National Landscapes* encyclopedia. Nothing stayed cheerful but the colors.

GOODY BAGS

Everyone in the class was looking forward to Naama's birthday party. Her parties always involved something really special. Two years ago, it was at the national park and they played Scavenger Hunt in paddleboats, and last year they had it at Skate Land, and the national skating champion, who was her dad's friend too, came and handed out autographs. Naama's father is a very important person who always wears expensive clothes and a tie, and carries a briefcase. Rafi said he was like a prime minister or a member of the Knesset, but that couldn't be, because he looked so young and you can't be in the Knesset till you're old. He's really nice, Naama's dad, and always has this big smile on his face, and he's blond too, and he always has jokes to tell, or scary stories. Naama told me once—it's a secret—how her dad goes to other countries a lot, but not just to ordinary places like France or London. He goes to secret countries, they're called stuff like Colombia and Magadascar . . . special places. He does important things there and they pay him a million billion for it, and all his friends from his job talk in funny languages and bring

Naama lots of presents. My dad isn't secret at all. He's got a shoe store on Herzl Street, and his friends talk Hebrew, and they never bring me presents. All they do is whack me on the shoulder till it hurts and tell me I'm a big man now or ask me how it's going at school, stupid stuff like that.

This year Naama's birthday party was at her house. She's got a cool house with three floors and a swimming pool with a waterslide and a separate gate for the car, the kind you open with a remote. And Naama's dad was really cool and he let us open and close the gate. And when Yuval and Miron pushed Elad the nerd into the pool and he climbed out all wet, Naama's dad laughed with everyone and didn't start lecturing us like my dad, who's always telling us to stop fooling around. And then he asked their Finippino housekeeper to bring the refreshments because the sun was out, and there were two clowns who had this great show they did and organized all these different contests. Naama told me as a secret how Shimon Peres was coming later, and maybe also Uri Geller, from TV, who'd known her dad since they were in high school. And the Finippino brought in a big, big birthday cake with sparklers on top. Naama showed me the rest of the house. They have three toilets, and every one of them is as big as our bathroom at home. And there's a fountain next to each of them that you could turn on and watch, so you don't get bored when you're taking a shit.

————

On our way back to the yard, I saw Naama's dad standing there in the doorway talking with two men. There was a cigarette in his mouth, and he looked sick and kind of sad. "Could you just wait another ten minutes? My daughter's having a birthday party. I'll just tell the kids that the party's ending early . . . I wouldn't want to ruin her day."

The men in the doorway nodded, and the fatter one said, "Okay. You have ten minutes. We'll be waiting in the car."

Naama and I sneaked back into the yard. Elad was there, even wetter than before. Miron had thrown him back into the water. They'd almost finished the cake; only some crumbs were left. Naama's dad came out into the yard. He had sweat on his forehead, but otherwise he seemed better than before and he was laughing again and smiling. And then the Finippino came out carrying a tray with lots of goody bags, the kind that have pictures of Popeye on them. We didn't want to take any at first, because goody bags are for little kids. But Naama's dad said they weren't ordinary goodie bags and that there was magic inside, which he'd brought from the other side of the world. What you had to do was take the bag home without opening it, put it under your pillow at night, and think really hard about the present you wanted to get more than anything else. The next morning you were supposed to bring it back without opening it, and tell Naama's dad what present you'd wished for. And Naama's dad would bring the bag to his personal magician, who would pull the presents out of the bags. Then on Saturday we'd all go over to their house and our presents would be there waiting for us. We all grabbed the bags, and Naama's dad reminded us not to show the bags to anyone and not to peek, because otherwise the magic would get out.

Walking out of Naama's house on our way home, I waved nicely at the people in the car, who'd agreed to wait an extra ten minutes so we could get our presents. Miron had filled a bag with water and wanted to throw it at the car, but Mickey talked him out of it. So Miron threw it at Elad instead. Elad said it was all bull, there was no such thing as magic and that he was just going to open his bag right now to see what it had inside. Miron grabbed the bag out of his hand and said that if Elad wanted to waste the magic, he'd take the bag away from him so he could get two presents. Elad cried and wanted his bag back, and Miron slapped him and said that if Elad told his parents or anything, he'd really let him have it.

Tonight I'll put the bag under my pillow and dream about an Alba skateboard. And even if there's no magic, I'll get it as a present, because Naama told me as a secret how you could always count on her dad.

MY BEST FRIEND

My best friend pissed on my door last night. I live in a fourth-floor walk-up. Dogs do that sometimes, to mark territory, to keep other males away. But he's no dog, he's my best friend. And besides, it's not his territory, it's the door to my apartment.

A few minutes earlier, my best friend had been waiting for the bus. He didn't know what to do. Slowly his bladder started to get the better of him. He tried to fight it, reminding himself the bus would be there any minute, except that was what he'd reminded himself twenty minutes before. Then it suddenly occurred to him that I, his best friend, lived just a few blocks away, at 14 Zamenhoff, in a fourth-floor walk-up. He left the bus stop and took off walking toward my apartment. Not exactly walking, really, more like half-running, then he broke into a sprint. And with every step he had a harder time holding it in, till he thought of sneaking into someone's back yard and peeing against a wall or a tree or a gas tank. He was less than fifty meters away from my house when he got that idea, but it struck him as both crude, in a certain way, and wussified. There are a lot of bad things you can say about my best friend, but one thing he's not is a wuss. So he forced himself to go another fifty meters and then started climbing the four floors to my place. With every step his bladder was getting bigger and bigger, like a balloon about to burst.

When he finally made it up all the stairs, he knocked on my door, then he rang the bell. Then knocked again. Hard. I wasn't home. Now of all times, in his hour of need, I, his best friend, had forsaken him for some pub—was doubtless hanging out at the bar, hitting on any girl unlucky enough to swim into my ken. There my best friend stood at my door, in desperation. He'd trusted me blindly, and now it was too late. He'd never make it all the way down those four flights of stairs. The only thing left to do, afterward, was leave me a crumpled note that read: "Sorry."

The moment she saw the puddle, the girl who'd agreed to come home with me that night had second thoughts. "Number one," she said, "it's gross. I'm not stepping in that. Number two, even if you mop it up, it will have stunk up the whole house. And number three," she added with an ever-so-slight curl of the lip, "if your best friend pisses on your door, that says something." After a brief silence, she clarified: "About you." And after another silence: "Not something good." Then she left.

She's the one who mentioned that this is how dogs mark territory. When she said it, she paused a little after the word *dog*, and gave me a meaningful look, from which I was supposed to deduce that my best friend had a lot in common with a dog. After that look, she left. I brought a floor rag from the kitchen porch, and a pail of water, and as I mopped it up, I hummed "We Shall Overcome." I was so proud of not having slapped her.

BOOMERANG

Sometimes Dad would leave the house for a few days, pack some things in a brown plastic bag that said Adidas and disappear.

Where'd Dad go? I'd ask Mom. "To the Dead Sea," she'd answer impatiently. What's he doing in the Dead Sea? "Ach, you're full of questions today," Mom would say. She'd be mad. "Go do your homework."

So I asked Dad. "Where am I going?" Dad would say. "I don't really remember. Where did Mom say I'm going?" To the Dead Sea. "Oh, yeah. Now I remember," Dad said, and he smiled. "That's where I'm going. The Dead Sea." What are you going to do at the Dead Sea? "What did Mom say I'm going to do?" Dad asked. I shrugged. She wouldn't tell me. Is it a secret? "Of course it's a secret," Dad whispered. "It's top secret. But you know what, I'll whisper it in your ear if you swear not to tell." I swear. "It's not enough just to say 'I swear,'" Dad said. "You have to swear on something." Okay, so I swear on my mother. "Your mother?" Dad said, laughing. "Okay, for what it's worth. Come here." I went over to him, and he whispered in my ear, "I'm going to the Dead Sea to fish." To fish? "Sssh . . ." Dad put his hand over my mouth. "Not out loud." But how can you fish? You don't have a rod. "Rods are for pussies," Dad said. "I catch the fish with my hands." What are pussies? And what do you do with the fish after you catch them? And why do you even go fishing? Dad's face got serious. "Those are really very good questions," he said, "but I can't answer them. Except the one about pussies. The others are just too secret." But I won't tell anyone. I swear on Mom and on Tsiyon too. "On Tsiyon too?" Dad asked, and he whistled. "On Tsiyon Shemesh?" I nodded. "Well, now I'm sure you won't tell," Dad said. "But they could kidnap you and inject you full of truth serum that'll suck all the secrets out of your head before you even know what's going on." Who? I asked. Who do you mean? "The pussies," Dad whispered. Mom came in. "When are you heading out?" she asked, lighting a cigarette. "Now," he said, picking up his bag. "Don't forget," he said, and he winked, putting his finger on his lips. "Not a word!" he said. Not a word, I won't say a word, even if they pump me full of all the serum in the world. "What serum?" Mom asked, looking hard at my father. "What kind of junk are you filling the kid's head with?" "Not even to Mom," Dad said with a laugh, and he left. I knew he trusted me.

Two days after Dad went away, Mickey came. Mickey always came when Dad went away. Most of the time, he came very late at night, when he thought I was sleeping, and stayed over. Tsiyon Shemesh said he was probably fucking my mother. Tsiyon's four years older than me and knows about things like that. So what should I do? I asked him. "Nothing," he said, "that's just how women are. They always want a dick, and a dick is a boomerang." Why? Why do they always want it? "That's just how it is," Tsiyon said. "Women are whores. It's their nature. Even my mother's like that." But why is a dick a boomerang? And what does that have to do with their being whores? "What do I know?" said Tsiyon. "My brother always says that. I think it means there's nothing you can do about it." So nothing's what I did.

I always hated Mickey. I don't know why, even though when he came in the morning, he brought me chocolate. He was always trying to make friends. "What's happening, big guy?" Mickey said when I opened the door. "Is your mom home?" I nodded. "And your dad?" he asked, looking around the apartment. No. "Where is he?" he asked, still looking around. "On a trip?" That's when I started to get suspicious. If he came to fuck Mom, then how come he's asking about Dad? I didn't say anything. Mom came out of the kitchen, Mickey put his black leather bag on the floor and went over to her. She was awfully surprised to see him. "What are you doing here?" she asked. "Are you crazy?" "I told my wife I was going to the hospital," Mickey said. "I had to see you." "Are you crazy?" Mom asked again. "What if Menachem was here?" "I would've said I was bringing you your medicine," Mickey said. "What's the problem?" He went over to Mom and grabbed her hand. "Can't a doctor visit his patient?" Mom tried to pull her hand away, but not really. He didn't let go. "What about the kid?" she asked in a whisper. "The kid?" Mickey said. "I brought him some chocolate."

When they went into the bedroom and closed the door, I opened his bag. There were all kinds of bottles and papers, but way down on the bottom, in a secret pocket, was the needle with the serum. My hands were shaking, but I picked it up and ran to the bedroom door. It was locked and I started banging. Mom, Mom, be careful! I yelled, don't tell him anything. After a while, Mom opened the door, all out of breath. "What's wrong?" she asked. She was very mad, I could tell. It's Mickey, I shouted, he doesn't really want to fuck you. He's an undercover pussy! Here's the needle, he had it in his bag. Don't tell him anything. *Don't tell!* Now Mom looked scared, and Mickey came to the door too. "Why do you make up all that crap?" Mom yelled. She grabbed me by the shoulders and shook me. I didn't make it up, Dad told me. That's when I started to cry. "Dad? Where is he?" Mickey asked. I won't tell you even if you kill me, you pussy. Mickey grabbed his bag and took off, his shoes in his hand, his shirt un-buttoned. The needle stayed with me. Mom tried to grill me later, but I kept quiet because I could see she didn't know about the pussies, and I knew Dad didn't want to tell her, and that pretty much fit in with what Tsiyon Shemesh said about women, about their nature and how they always want a boomerang. When Dad came back, Mom talked to him for a while and he was really mad at her for letting a pussy in the house. I know, on account of he slapped her and threw his brown bag out the win-dow. I didn't hear exactly what they said because they closed the door, but after that, he didn't go away anymore. That night, he told me that himself. "I can't leave your mother alone for a minute," he said. But what about the fish? "What fish?" You know, Dad, the fish in the Dead Sea. "Give it a rest with the questions!" he said. "Go do your homework."

SO GOOD

Wearing nothing but pajama bottoms and cowboy boots, Itzik sat on the edge of the bed and stared out the window. The sun was shining out there. He felt like a jerk. Happiness was supposed to arrive today. His sources had just informed him about it five minutes ago, and here he was, sitting on the bed like an idiot, not doing a thing about it. He thought back over the last time Happiness had come—how his father had opened the door for it, just like that, and how Itzik himself, a pale-faced little boy, had sat there at the kitchen table making paper collages, not afraid of anything.

He started to tremble. "It can't get in," he whispered. "No matter what." If only he could keep it from getting inside, everything would be okay. He lunged at the dresser and started pushing it toward the door. Once he'd blocked the entrance completely, he got out his hunting rifle and began shoving the cartridges into it. This time, he'd be ready. Not like at his parents' house. Nobody was going to turn him into a grinning zombie who loved daytime TV and García Márquez, and kissed his mother every chance he got. "Where's my flak jacket?" he yelled to no one. "Where's my flak jacket, son of a bitch." He rummaged frantically through the cabinet under the sink till he found it, then put on an undershirt and the jacket. Next he stuck the ice picks and Stanley knives into the fireplace, with the blades pointing straight up. If they're so smart, let them try the chimney. He'd teach them a thing or two about Happiness. Five years he'd done at Club Med. Five years, damn them to hell. With the girl he loved, with sex both oral and anal, with money to spend like there was no tomorrow. He'd had it real bad. He knew it for what it was. If Grandma hadn't died, he'd still be there now.

The first to arrive was Opportunity. They always sent her in first, like some goddamn Bedouin scout. Probably figured she was expendable. She knocked at the door, then tried the handle, which was electrified. The shock stunned her to the ground. That's when Itzik broke the window with the rifle butt and stuck the barrel out. "Think of something nice," he muttered through clenched teeth and pressed the trigger. "Think of something nice, bitch, all the way up to Heaven. I'm not giving in without a fight. I'm not my father. I won't let you drag me away in some van festooned with Walt Disney characters and a shit-eating grin on my face." He pumped another slug into blank-faced Opportunity just to be on the safe side.

Suddenly he remembered what Greenberg had said about the fast one they pulled using cable TV. Son of a bitch. Here he was, sitting around like a jive rookie, with his back to the Family Channel, as if he'd never heard about what NBC did to the Depression Underground in Seattle back in '87. How stupid could he be! He spun around and fired another one into the TV, a split second before Cosby kissed Lisa. "Gotta stay cool," he muttered under his breath. "Gotta stay cool, no matter what happens."

He was just beginning to focus on Somalia when he heard rustling in the bushes. It was Sheer Enjoyment with the take-away pizzas and the porn magazines, inching her way along the hedge. He couldn't quite get her in his sights. But she didn't try to get any closer.

"Hey, babe, I hate my pizzas cold," he screamed. But she didn't even answer. The helicopters were overhead now, with their enormous loudspeakers booming techno hits and schmaltzy crooners at top volume. He put his hands over his ears and con-centrated on Holocaust Memorial Day, on women with a breast cut off, on homeless people shivering in the New York winter. He did have a hint of a smile on his face, but the music remained on the outside. Still, there was something going on. It all seemed too easy. The helicopters. Sheer Enjoyment not making a move. It had to be a ploy. "The roof, damn it," he blurted. "It's got to be up on the roof." He took a few potshots through the shingles. Something fell down the chimney straight onto the spikes. That was Success! She was holding a packet of winning lottery tickets. Itzik doused her with gasoline and threw his Zippo into the fire-place. The body caught fire instantly. Along with the winning tickets. The flames lapped them up long before they had a chance to spread through the cabin. Smoke was filling the room, mixed with another smell, the fragrance of hot corn on the cob, of old-fashioned ice cream, of Mom tucking him in at night. Gas. He crawled along the floor, trying to get to the gas masks. AIDS, he thought to himself. People abusing children all over the world at this very moment. Children. So sweet, I'd love to have some of my own, and a wife. Who loves me. Being tortured in the Security Service dungeons—he tried. No way. The smile just kept spreading. Threatening to swallow him up. Three emotions he couldn't quite make out were taking over, removing his flak jacket, wiping the number off his arm with saliva. Replacing his "Why?" undershirt with a "Don't Worry, Be Happy" one. Don't lose hope, it'll work out, he said, trying to cheer himself up as they dragged him outside. She'll be there, waiting for you. You'll have an amazing future. You'll have an APV minivan. So intense was the anticipation that his knees were turning to mush. You'll have it so good, you lucky son of a bitch, you don't know how good.

By then the tears in his throat had dried up. The trees outside were all green. And the sky was bright blue. The weather was just right, not too warm and not too cold. A van covered with *Simpsons* characters and mortgage ads was there already, waiting for him at the bottom of the stairs.

RAISING THE BAR

When Nandy Schwartz, the German pole-vaulter, cleared the six-sixty mark on the second try, he wasn't thinking about anything. There was a lump in his throat the size of a billiard ball, and as his eyes followed his outstretched feet passing over the bar without touching it, he struggled hard to keep from crying. He sank into the mat below and was surprised at the enormous tears choking him while the announcer compared his record to that of the legendary Bob Beamon. "Everyone here today has just seen a piece of history," the megaphones crooned, and Nandy Schwartz, the only person in the stadium who hadn't really seen it, held his arm high for the cameras.

Nandy's answering machine had no outgoing message. It just beeped with laconic arrogance—which didn't stop the Kellogg's people from leaving three messages.

"Raising the bar" was their suggestion for the new campaign, starring Nandy. "Eight vitamins instead of six!"

Four hundred and ninety thousand dollars in the bank. Nandy didn't hear the messages. He happened to be in the shower stall, curled up in a fetal position on the tiles, letting the hot water scald his back. The steam seeped from his boiled pores as if from a rusty kettle while he lay there with his thumb in his mouth, urinating into the stream of water, watching the yellow urine swirl toward the drain. Those 490,000 dollars could fix him up, except that unfortunately he was already fixed up in his split-level five-room apartment in northern Bonn. Down on the tiles a piece of history was cooking away, sucking the memory of many triumphs from a thumb. Money, fame, and health aside, he'd had sixty-three girls, each with her own story. Some with more than one. If he wanted to raise the bar any higher, he'd have to find a professor at least fifty-four years old, and if he wanted it lower, he'd need a retard under sixteen.

VLADIMIR HUSSEIN

S on of a bitch," the fat guy muttered and banged his fist on the bus stop bench. Vladimir kept looking at the pictures in the newspaper, taking no notice at all of the words around them. Time was moving slowly. Vladimir hated waiting for buses. "Son of a bitch," the fat guy said again, loudly this time, and spat on the sidewalk close to Vladimir's feet. "Are you talking to me?" Vladimir asked, a bit surprised, and looked up from the paper to meet the fat guy's alcohol-glazed eyes. "No, I'm talking to my ass," the fat guy yelled. "Oh," Vladimir said and went back to the paper. In it was a color picture of piles of hacked-up bodies in the city hall square. Vladimir continued to browse his way to the sports section. "Damn right I'm talking to you, asshole." The fat guy got up and stood over Vladimir. "Oh," Vladimir said, "that's what I thought at first, but you said—" "Forget what I said, you dirty Arab." "Russian," Vladimir said, quick to hide behind the branch of his family not presently under attack. "My mother's from Riga." "Sure she is," the fat guy said unbelievingly. "And your father?" "From Nablus," Vladimir admitted and went back to the paper. "Two diseases in one body," the fat guy said. "What are they going to think of next to steal our jobs." There was a picture in the newspaper of charred Kurdish midgets popping out of a huge toaster, and the inquisitive Vladimir was sorry for a moment that he'd sworn not to read captions.

"Get up," the fat guy said. Vladimir finally reached the sports section he was so eager to get to and saw a picture of a black player hanging from a basketball hoop. Vladimir couldn't resist the temptation and peeked at the caption: "Frustrated Fans Demand New Blood." "I told you to get up," the fat guy repeated. "Me?" Vladimir asked, "not your—" "Yes, you," the fat guy said. Vladimir got up. The black guy in the picture had played two seasons with North Carolina College before getting hanged on a Tel Aviv court, so Vladimir learned as he stood up, violating another one of his principles. It was five o'clock and the bus still hadn't come. In his radio speech, the Prime Minister had promised rivers of blood, and the fat guy was a head taller than him. Vladimir kneed him in the balls, then smashed him with the iron crowbar he'd stashed in the newspaper. The fat guy fell down and started wailing, "Arabs! Russians! Help!" Vladimir gave him another whack on the head with the crowbar and sat back down on the bench.

The bus arrived at 5:07. "What's with him?" the driver asked, jerking his head in the direction of the fat guy, who was sprawled on the sidewalk. "He's not coming," Vladimir said. "I can see that," the driver said, "but shouldn't we help him or something?" "He's epileptic," Vladimir said. "Better not touch him." "If he's epileptic, where's all the blood coming from?" the driver asked. Vladimir shrugged. "From the Prime Minister's speech on the radio." He put his monthly bus pass in his pocket and sat down in the back next to an old man wearing a beret and glasses, doing a crossword puzzle. "Bulbul," the old man said. "A songbird (six letters)," Vladimir recited loudly. "Who's talking to you, you dirty Arab?" the old man said. "Border Patrol policemen's favorite statement/question (twenty-eight letters, not including the apostrophe)," Vladimir said without hesitation. "Not bad for a *schvartze*," the old man mumbled admiringly. "I love crossword puzzles," Vladimir said, lowering his head modestly.

When they reached Vladimir's stop, the old man took off his beret and tore out the string that dangled from the back of it. "Here, young man, a gift from me," he said, handing Vladimir the hat. "Thank you, Gramps," Vladimir said, took the beret, and hopped onto the sidewalk. The bus pulled away, and Vladimir instinctively tossed the hat into the green trash can and dropped to the ground. The explosion came a few seconds later, showering him with garbage.

He hurried to the marble-façade building where he lived with his family, took the stairs two at a time, and reached the roof panting. Grandma Natasha was sitting in the tent watching public service announcements on TV. They were showing a blond model in a bikini doing the backstroke in a river of blood flowing along Arlozorov Street. "She's not a real blonde," Grandma Natasha grumbled, pointing at the model. "She has it bleached." Vladimir's mother came into the tent carrying a laundry basket. "Where were you?" she asked angrily. "We've been looking for you all morning. Those antipollution lunatics crucified Grandpa in the central bus station." Vladimir was picturing himself fucking the TV model. "I want you at the funeral, not like at your father's, when you ran away, do you hear me?" He didn't care if her hair was bleached, he liked her. "Vladimir? Are you even listening to me?" Getting mad, his mother started cursing in Russian. "Are you talking to me?" Vladimir asked and looked at her for a minute. "No, I'm talking to God," his mother said and went back to cursing. "Oh," Vladimir said and went back to watching TV. They were showing the bottom half of the model's body now. The shiny blood flowed around it without sticking to it. There was a caption and the city's logo above it, but Vladimir was able to resist the temptation and avoid reading it.

KNOCKOFF VENUS

The gods had their dignity. When they got here, everyone wanted to help them: the Jewish Agency, the Ministry of Immigrant Absorption, the Housing Ministry. Everyone. But they fended for themselves. They came with nothing, they asked for nothing, they worked like Arabs and were satisfied. And so Mercury wound up in deliveries, Atlas in moving, and Vulcan in a garage. Venus came to our office. She Xeroxed.

I was going through a rough patch. I didn't know what to do with myself. I was alone, completely alone. I was desperate to have a great love. Usually, when I'm in that state, I take up a hobby—painting, the guitar, whatever. Then, if I can get into it, it makes me feel better and I forget that I don't have anyone in the world, but that time, I knew no macramé course could help me. I needed something I could believe in. A great love that would never go away, that would never leave me. My therapist listened with interest and suggested that I buy a dog. I left my therapist.

Venus worked from eight-thirty to six, sometimes later, Xeroxing reams and collating them into neat stacks. Even in that posi-

tion, sweaty and bent over the machine, wincing against the flash-
ing light, she was still the most beautiful thing I'd ever seen. I
wanted to say so, but I couldn't get up the nerve. In the end, I
wrote it down on a piece of paper and left it on her desk. The next
morning, the note was waiting for me, along with fifty copies.

Her Hebrew wasn't great. She was a goddess, but she was
making seven thousand shekels, pretax. I know because once,
when I was down in Accounting, I looked at her paycheck. I
wanted to marry her, I wanted to save her. I was positive she
could save me. I don't know how I did it, but finally I asked her
to a movie. The girl chosen by Paris as most beautiful of the
goddesses smiled the gentlest, shyest smile you can imagine and
said yes.

Before I left the house, I looked in the mirror. There was a zit
on my forehead. The Roman goddess of beauty and I are going
to a movie tonight, I said to myself, the Roman goddess of
beauty and I are going out on a date. I popped it and toilet-
papered off the greasy blood. Who are you, pathetic mortal, that
you want to buy her popcorn, that you dare put your arm
around her in the shadows of a cineplex?

After the movie, we went to get a drink. I was hoping she
wouldn't talk to me about the plot. I had no idea what had happened on-screen. I'd been looking at her all through the movie.
We talked some about the office and about how her family was
adapting to Israel. She liked it here. Of course she wanted more
out of life, that would come, but in the meantime it was just so
good to be here she had no complaints. Oh, God, she said,
touching my arm, you have no idea what an awful time we had,
back there.

Driving her home, I asked if she believed in God. She laughed. If you're asking whether I know that he exists, she said, then the answer's yes. Not just him, a whole bunch. If you're asking whether I believe in him, then no, definitely not.

Before I knew it we were at her house and she'd already popped the car door. I cursed myself for taking the short route. I wanted so much for her to stay with me a little longer. I prayed for a miracle. For the police to stop us, for someone to kidnap us, for something to happen that would leave us together. Already out of the car, she asked me up for coffee.

She's sleeping now, next to me, in bed. Lying on her stomach, her head sunk into the pillow. Her lips move slightly, as if speaking to herself silently. Her right arm is curled around me, her hand resting on my chest. I try not to breathe more than I have to so my chest rising and falling won't wake her up. She's beautiful. Beyond beautiful. Perfect. And pretty nice, too.

Tomorrow I'm buying a dog.

ATONEMENT

Right to his face she said it, on the synagogue steps. The
moment they'd walked out, even before he'd had a
chance to put the yarmulke back in his pocket. She made
him let go of her hand and told him he was an animal, he'd better not talk that way to her ever again, dragging her out of there
like she was some kind of property. And she said it out loud, too.
People could hear. People he worked with, even the rabbi, but
that didn't stop her from raising her voice. He should've slapped
her right then and there, should've shoved her right down the
stairs. But like an idiot, he waited till they got home. And then,
when he beat her, she seemed so taken aback. Like a dog that
you hit for shitting on the carpet when so much time has passed
the shit's already dry. He kept at it, smacking her across the face,
and she shouted, "Menachem, Menachem!" as if the person
beating her was some stranger and she was crying out for him to
come and save her. "Menachem, Menachem!" She cringed in the
corner. "Menachem, Menachem." And he gave her a kick in the
ribs.

When he laid off and lit a cigarette, he noticed the spot of blood on his synagogue shoes, and he looked at her again and saw a red crescent on the dress he'd bought her for the holidays. The crescent kept growing fuller. She must have been bleeding from the nose. He pulled up a dining room chair and sat down with his back to her, facing the electric clock. Behind him he could hear her crying. He could hear the moans as she kept trying to get back on her feet, the thumps as she fell back into her corner. The hands of the electric clock were moving at an alarming speed, and he loosened his belt and tilted his body forward.

"I'm sorry," he heard her whimper from the corner. "I'm sorry, Menachem. I didn't mean it, really, forgive me." And he forgave her and so did God, and the timing was truly perfect, with only thirty seconds to go.

PATIENCE

T he most patient man in the world was sitting on a bench next to Dizengoff Center. No one was sitting on the bench beside him, not even pigeons. The perverts in the public toilets were making such loud, weird noises that you couldn't ignore them. The most patient man in the world was holding a newspaper in his hand, pretending to read.

He wasn't really reading, he was waiting for something. No one knew what.

A German tabloid offered ten thousand euros to anyone who found out what the man was waiting for, but no one did. In the exclusive interview he agreed to give to a CNN correspondent, the most patient man in the world said he was waiting for lots of things, but that wasn't the place to list them. "So where *is* the place?" the persistent journalist asked, but the most patient man in the world didn't answer, he just waited quietly for the next question. He waited and waited and waited, until finally they cut back to the studio.

People from all over the world made pilgrimages to ask what his secret was. Hyperactive brokers, hysterical students, artists desperate for their promised fifteen minutes of fame. The most patient man in the world didn't know exactly what he was supposed to tell them. "Shave," he always ended up saying, "shave with hot water. It's very soothing." And all the men would rush right off to their bathrooms and nick their faces in a thousand places. Women said he was a chauvinist. They said his macho answer automatically denied every woman her right to attain a state of calm. Women also found him very ugly. Laurie Anderson actually wrote a song about him. "A Very Patient, Ugly Chauvinist" was the name of the song. "His biological clock is taking its time" was the chorus.

The most patient man in the world fell asleep on the bench with his eyes half closed. In his dreams, meteors crashed into the ground with the faint sound of buses hitting their brakes, hideous volcanoes erupted with the sound of perverts flushing toilets, and the girl he'd loved for many years told her husband she was leaving him with the cooing of birds. Four meters away, two pigeons were trying to peck out each other's eyes for no reason. They weren't even fighting over food. "Shave," the man said in his sleep. "Shave with hot water. It's very soothing."

GAZA BLUES

Weismann had a rasping, dry cough, the hack of a tubercular, and the whole way there he kept coughing, and spitting into some tissues.

"It's the cigarettes," he apologized. "They're killing me." When we got to the Erez roadblock, we parked at the gas station. There was a taxi waiting for us there with local plates. "Did you remember to bring the forms?" Weismann asked and spat a yellow gob on the sidewalk.

I nodded.

"How about the powers of attorney?"

I said yes, those too.

We didn't have to tell the driver what to do. He knew to take us straight to Fadid's office. It was already late May, but the streets were flooded. Must have been some problem with the sewers.

"Shitty road," the driver complained. "Every three week, tires finish." I figured he was getting ready to hike the fare.

We walked into Fadid's office, and he shook our hands. "Let

me introduce you," Weismann said. "This is Niv, an associate in our firm. He's here to learn."

"Keep your eyes open, Niv," Fadid said in perfect Hebrew. "Keep your eyes peeled and look around. You'll learn plenty." Fadid led us into his office. "You sit here," he told Weismann, pointing to the leather chair behind the desk. "And this"—he pointed to a small wooden stool in the corner—"this is for the interpreter. I'll be back at two. Make yourselves at home."

I sat down on the leather couch and laid out the forms in five separate piles on the low table beside me. Meanwhile, the interpreter showed up. "There are five cases," he said. His name was Mas'oud or something like Mas'oud. "Two eye, two leg, one ball." From the way Weismann had described it, it wouldn't take more than twenty minutes each to take the depositions, which meant in an hour and a half we'd be heading back.

Weismann asked the usual questions through the interpreter, lighting each cigarette with the last. I had them sign the medical secrecy waivers and powers of attorney, and explained to each of them through the interpreter that if they won we'd take a cut from fifteen to twenty percent, depending. One of them, a half-blind woman, signed with her thumb, like in the movies. The guy who got it in the balls asked in Hebrew, when I'd finished explaining, if the Security Service guy who kicked his balls in would wind up in jail if we won. "I know his name. I say it in court," he said. "Steve, *in'al abu*, that was his name."

The interpreter told him off in Arabic for talking Hebrew. "If you want to talk with them yourself," he said, "you don't need me. I can wait outside."

I know a little Arabic. Took it in high school.

An hour and ten minutes later we were back in the taxi already, and on our way to the Erez roadblock. Fadid had invited us for lunch, but Weismann said we were in a hurry. Weismann didn't stop coughing and spitting into his tissues the whole way back.

"It's no good, mister," the driver told him. "You need doctor. My sister husband he doctor. Live near here."

"No thanks, I'm okay. I'm used to it." Weismann tried to smile at him. "It's all on account of the cigarettes. They're doing me in."

We hardly spoke the whole way home. I was thinking about my five o'clock basketball practice. "In three of the cases, we stand a chance," Weismann said. "The one with the balls, forget it. Three years he spent in jail after the interrogation, not once did he say he'd been injured. How can you prove they did it to him three and a half years ago?"

"But you're taking him on all the same?"

"Yeah," Weismann mumbled. "I didn't say I wouldn't take him on. I just said we don't stand a chance." He kept fiddling with the radio dial, trying to pick up something, but all he got was static. After that he tried humming something, but a few seconds later he got bored, lit up, and started coughing again. Then he asked me once more if I'd remembered to have them sign everything.

I said I had.

"You know what." He turned to me suddenly. "I should have been born black. Every time I come out of there I tell myself: 'Weismann, you should have been born black.' Not here. Someplace far away. Like New Orleans." He opened the car window and flicked out the cigarette. "Billy, that's what my name should have been. Billy White. That's a good name for a singer." He cleared his throat as though he were about to start singing, but the moment he inhaled, he started up coughing and wheezing.

"See this?" he said when he was finished and held the used tissue, the one he'd coughed into, up close to my face. "Now here's a little something that I made up all by myself. It's the real thing, isn't it? Billy White and the Dismals, that's what they'd call us. We'd do nothing but blues."

THE SUMMER OF '76

In the summer of '76, they remodeled our house and added another bathroom. That was my mother's private bathroom, with green tiles, white curtains, and a kind of small drawing board she could put on her knees to do crossword puzzles on. The door of this new bathroom had no lock because it was my mother's and no one else was allowed to go in anyway. We were very happy that summer. My sister, who was best friends with Rina Mor, that year's Miss Universe, married a nice South African dentist who'd immigrated to Israel, and they moved to Raanana. My older brother finished the army and got a job as a security guard for El Al. My father made a pile on oil-drilling stocks and became a partner in an amusement park. And I made them all bring me presents.

"Different people—different dreams," that's what was written on the American catalog I picked my surprises from. It had everything from a gun that shot potatoes to life-size Spider-Man dolls. And every time my brother flew to America, he let me pick one thing from the catalog. The kids in the neighborhood looked up to me because of my new toys, and they listened to me about everything. On Friday afternoons, my whole class used to go to the park to play baseball with the bat and glove my brother brought me. And I was the biggest champion, because Jeremy, my sister's husband, taught me to throw curveballs that no one could lay a bat on.

Terrible things could happen around me, but they never even touched me. In the Baltic Sea, three sailors ate their captain; the mother of a kid in my school had a boob cut off; Dalit's brother was killed in a training accident in the army. Anat Moser, the prettiest girl in class, said yes, she'd be my girlfriend, and she didn't even talk it over with the other girls. My brother said he was just waiting for my birthday to take me on a trip to America as a gift. Meanwhile, on Saturdays, he'd drive me and Anat to the amusement park in his Swedish car and I'd tell the park operators that I was Schwartz's son and they'd let us go on all the rides for free.

On holidays, we'd go to visit Grandpa Reuven in Zichron, and when he shook my hand, he'd squeeze it so hard I cried. Then he'd yell at me that I was spoiled and needed to learn to shake hands like a man. He'd always tell my mother she was bringing me up all wrong, that she wasn't preparing me for life. Mom would always apologize and say that actually, she *was* preparing me, it was just that life today wasn't anything like life used to be. That today, you didn't have to know how to make Molotov cocktails from alcohol and nails or how to kill for bread. It was enough to learn how to enjoy life. But Grandpa wouldn't let it go. He'd pinch my ear and whisper that if you want to know how to enjoy life, you also have to know what sadness is. Otherwise, it isn't worth a damn. I tried, but life was so beautiful then, that summer of '76, that no matter how hard I worked at it, I couldn't be sad about anything.

TRANSLATION ACKNOWLEDGMENTS

"Asthma," "Atonement," "Cheerful Colors," "Cramps," "Crazy Glue," "Gaza Blues," "Goody Bags," "Gulliver in Icelandic," "Happy Birthday to You," "Hat Trick," "Journey," "Monkey Say, Monkey Do," "Moral Something," "My Best Friend," "The Night the Buses Died," "A No-Magician Birthday," "Nothing," "Painting," "Quanta," "Raising the Bar," "The Real Winner of the Preliminary Games," "Sidewalks," "Slimy Shlomo Is a Homo," "So Good," "Vacuum Seal," and "World Champion" were translated by Miriam Shlesinger.

"Alternative," "The Backgammon Monster," "Boomerang," "An Exclusive," "Freeze!," "The Girl on the Fridge," "Knockoff Venus," "Loquat," "Myth Milk," "No Politics," "Not Human Beings," "One Hundred Percent," "On the Nutritional Value of Dreams," "Patience," "The Summer of '76," "Terminal," "Through Walls," "Vladimir Hussein," "Without Her," and "Yordan" were translated by Sondra Silverston.